Dustbin Cat

From The Chicken House

I love my cat. Of course, she fights sometimes,
and even 'caterwauls' at night, but cats are cats,
and have to be appreciated for what they are.
They live alongside us and deserve a place in
our world even if sometimes we have to stand
up for them against prejudice and cruelty.
That's what she told me to say, anyway!

Barry Cunningham
Publisher

2 Palmer Street, Frome, Somerset BA11 1DS

Dustbin
Cat

INGRID LEE

First published in Great Britain in 2010
The Chicken House
2 Palmer Street
Frome, Somerset BA11 1DS
United Kingdom
www.doublecluck.com

Cover and interior design by Steve Wells
Typeset by Dorchester Typesetting Group Ltd
Printed and bound in Great Britain by CPI Bookmarque, Croydon, CR0 4TD

The paper used in this Chicken House book is made from wood grown
in sustainable forests.

1 3 5 7 9 10 8 6 4 2

British Library Cataloguing in Publication data available.

ISBN 978-1-906427-53-5

For AL
Cat Friend

Cat lady

May 25

Police were called to the home of Mary Downs last evening. Neighbours reported hearing strange cries inside.

Mrs Downs was found semi-conscious in her bedroom. Cats roamed the place. 'Must have been fifty of 'em,' said the officer. 'The smell could have knocked you over.'

Most locals were shocked to discover that Mary Downs was a 'cat lady'.

'I thought there was something strange going on,' reported Joe Close, a resident on the street. 'Her house was spooky. I went over there a few times; offered to do some cleaning up. The old lady never cracked the door open an inch. I guess she didn't want anybody looking around.'

Animal Services have taken the cats to a local shelter. Some of the animals appear dehydrated. Five are pregnant. 'Looks like she collected strays,' said one official. 'We found eleven cats in the freezer. They died of natural causes.'

Mr Close thought otherwise. 'That Downs

woman probably stole the cats. You know how old people get – start acting weird. People like that should be in institutions.'

'I hear cats yowling around my bins at night,' added Ms April Winsome, another neighbour. 'They have eyes that look right through you.'

The feral problem will be discussed at the next town hall meeting. Some Clydesdale councillors have suggested that a round-up of the alley cats might . . .

*T*he cat prowled the house restlessly. She scratched at the windows and doors. When the new puppy stuck its chops into her flank, she hissed and swatted its nose. The puppy ran under the bed.

'The cat's at the puppy again,' the woman complained. 'Her mewling makes me crazy. There's hair everywhere. The furniture is all scratched up. I don't know why I ever wanted a cat.'

'Maybe I'll take the cat for a drive,' suggested her husband. 'I'll lose her down a country road. She can take up life on a farm. I don't want our little pup to grow up with a complex.'

The cat crouched on the passenger seat. Her amber eyes glittered in the dark.

After a while the car stopped, and the man got out. 'Scat!' he said. He tossed the cat into the scrub.

The cat watched the car lights fade into the distance. Her ears caught the night noises. An insect chirruped and a swift wing clipped the grass. Somewhere an owl hooted. The cat began to follow the highway, picking her way through the weedy verge.

Suddenly she sensed danger. A dark shadow plummeted towards the earth, a great feathery beast with sharp claws, and the cat veered helter-skelter on to the open road. When a tired truck driver barrelling along the white line sounded his horn, she flattened to the tarmac. The steel trailer skimmed over her back. Wind blasted her fur.

At the gas station on the outskirts of town, the cat turned on to High Street. An alleyway took her to the yard of an apartment block. There, under a budding lilac bush, she stopped to think.

Something was wrong. She was a housecat. She was used to a full bowl of food and a warm bed. Where was her home?

The eager yowl took her by surprise. Alert to this new danger, she peered between the branches into a pair of cold blue eyes. The grey tom wasted no time. He ran at her . . .

It was almost morning when the cat stumbled upon the coal cellar. She slipped between the rotten boards. At the bottom of the chute, she nested into the foam of an old car seat. All day long she waited for her owners to fetch her. Thin sticks of sunlight crisscrossed the dark sides of the chute – back and forth, back and forth. By the next night, one thing was clear.

She had waited for nothing.

The cat crept back to High Street as Paul Lacy hurried home for his dinner. Paul grinned when he saw her peeping around an alley bin. He stooped to grab a handful of gravel. Bingo! The first stone hit her right between the eyes. Paul laughed outright. That cat was a goner. 'Cat,' he yelled, taking chase. 'Say your prayers!' He hurled the rest of the ammo.

There was nothing at the end of the alley but a two-metre fence. Butt up to the boards, the cat whirled to face her attacker. Even though she dodged this way and that, a hailstorm of flinty bits scraped her tender skin. They stung her eyes. She sprung for the top of the fence. She had to escape.

A tired voice cut through the dark. 'Paul, is that you out there? It's past your bedtime. Get in the house right now. Don't make me send out your dad!'

The boy paused when he heard his mom. 'Cat,'

he promised. 'Looks like you got lucky. Next time I see you, I'll teach you good.' He grabbed a rock. 'Here's something so you don't forget.'

His parting shot split the cat's front paw right to the bone. She was so intent on escape, she barely noticed. She didn't stop running until she got back to the coal cellar. The pain caught up with her later. By morning, her eyes were swollen shut. Her body ached. And her paw was on fire. She needed water and she needed food. Slowly she made her way back up the steep coal chute, leaning into the curved wall for balance. The light of day was staggering after the darkness.

The cat hobbled along until she came to a stagnant ditch. She stopped to lap the murky water. There was a dead bird, and she tore at the flesh ravenously. It made her sick.

A woman pushed a carriage along the pavement, cooing at her baby in a soft voice. When the dirty creature with the runny eyes crossed her path, she was frightened. 'Horrid cat!' she cried. 'Get away from my baby.' She swung her bag.

The cat scurried back to the coal cellar. For hours she shivered. Mucus glued her eyes shut. Her insides churned. And her paw wouldn't hold her up. It was late afternoon by the time thirst drove her out of the cellar once again. She scurried through the yard to the main street. People moved out of her path. Some people even crossed the road.

Cats like that were bad luck.

The cat soldiered on blindly. She was so far gone, she walked right into Billy Reddick.

ONE

'I'm going to the corner shop,' Billy Reddick said. 'Can I have money for a coke?'

His mom looked up from her figures. 'I'm sorry, Billy. You know I don't have any. It'll be like this until I finish the course and find myself another job. There's juice in the fridge.'

Billy's dad walked in. When he saw the books and papers strewn over the table, his face got redder than a ripe tomato. 'This place is a mess,' he grunted. 'Least a man can do is come home to a tidy house. Seeing as you're a kept woman.'

Billy looked at his dad. 'Dad, can I have a dollar for a coke?'

His dad flipped a coin on the table. 'Sure, kid. Just remember where the money's coming from.' He dropped his toolbox on the table and looked at his wife. 'Time you started on dinner, Mae,' he said.

'Guess you know how to take out a frying pan, Walt,' Billy's mom shot back.

Their bickering didn't let up. Money was tight. Since his mom had lost her job and enrolled in some schooling, Billy's dad had a short fuse. Billy grabbed the dollar from his dad and took off.

The traffic on High Street was winding down for the day. Most of the shops drowsed in the spring sunshine. Even the newsagent was empty. Billy checked out a rack of old comics and drank his coke. He kept thinking about his folks. Sometimes his mom got so angry with his dad that she didn't speak to him for days. Other times his dad stayed out late. Billy couldn't stop thinking. What if one day his mother decided to do the leaving? What if one day she upped and disappeared?

The cat limping down the street took Billy by surprise. Most of the street cats around town kept out of sight. They did their roaming after dark. This one walked a crooked line down the pavement in broad daylight. Billy almost tripped over it.

Billy watched the cat crawl under some old boards stacked next to the chapel alley. It was a pretty ugly cat. The fur was powdered with black grime. Dried mucus zippered the eyes.

As he stood looking, an older boy in a ponytail and a City Hall shirt came out of the alley. The boy scowled at Billy before he hurried away. Billy eyed the little brick church. What was that guy doing around the back of it? No one had prayed in there for a long time. There were chains looped through the double doors. Dust dulled the stained-glass window in the gable, and the bell tower was boarded up. Even the bell inside was long gone.

Billy looked down at the boards again. He bent close and called, 'Cat. Hey, cat.'

The thing practically rushed into his arms.

Billy didn't know what to do. He stood up with his hands full of cat. Cat hair stuck to his shirt. Black powder smeared his skin. Billy looked around for some help. Folk hurrying by paid him no attention. They had their dinners to think about. He was just a dirty boy with a dirty cat.

The cat felt so light. Billy could feel its heart beating out of time. One paw was wet with infection, and the smell of it made him gag. He threw the cat down and shooed it away. 'Scat!' he said.

The cat crawled back under the boards. Billy stood there for a while longer before he went home. When he got up to the apartment, there was a note.

At the library. Meatloaf in the fridge.
Mom
xx

Billy went out again. Somehow he ended up back at the entrance to the chapel alley. 'Cat,' he called.

He bent down to the boards. 'Cat, you still there?'

Nothing.

Billy lifted one of the boards. The cat crouched in a damp heap. 'Look,' he explained. 'I'm sorry. My dad would never let me bring you home. He *hates* cats.'

The cat didn't seem to hear. It was so still. Billy didn't know what to do. Finally he put the board down and walked away. Maybe there was an early ball practice going on at the park. He was halfway down High Street before he changed his mind. There was something about that cat.

Back at the alley, Billy took one more look under the boards. The cat hadn't moved. 'Look cat,' he sighed. 'I suppose I could take you to the shelter. You aren't going to last much longer out here.'

The shelter wasn't far. A friend of Billy's had gone there for a dog once, and Billy had tagged along. He scooped up the cat, holding it so the wet paw didn't touch him. 'Where've you been?' he asked. He could see some lighter hair under the powder. 'That black stuff looks like coal dust. You been hiding in a coal bin?'

The cat hung limply in his arms. Maybe the sore foot was making it sick.

'What did you do?' Billy asked. His arms were getting stiff. 'Did you get hit by a rock? Stick your foot under some car?'

There was no answer.

It was just a dumb, dirty cat.

By the time he got to the animal shelter, it was closing time. The woman at the front desk wanted to get home to her kids. 'It's late,' she said when Billy walked in. 'Come back tomorrow.'

'I found a cat,' he said. 'There's something wrong with its paw.'

Just what I need now, the woman thought. 'Who owns it?'

'I don't know,' said Billy. 'It hasn't got a collar. I found it wandering down the street.'

The woman sighed. What a headache. The town was full of stray cats. The animal shelter had more cats than they had cages. And the complaints. Why, just that morning a man had come storming up to the front desk with a dead bird. 'It's a cardinal!' he had yelled. 'A female. The bird used to come late afternoon for the sunflower seeds. Now it's nothing but feather and bone.'

The man had tears in his eyes, he was so worked up. 'The wild cats are to blame – the feral ones. They probably got at the young in the nest, too. Those cats are killing machines. They see a bird and they have to have it. The city's got to get rid of them, I tell you – before there are no birds left to sing.'

The woman at the desk picked up an empty hamster cage. 'Well, thanks for bringing the cat by,' she told Billy. She eyed the thing with a tired frown. What was all that black stuff? 'We'll take care of it for you. Put it in here.'

Billy looked at the small wire cage. He looked at the dirty cat in his arms.

'What'll you do with it?' he asked.

'Look, kid,' the woman said bitterly. 'I've got to tell you. There are too many cats in this town. Anybody can see that this one's past redemption. We'll put it down. Best way to stop the hurting.'

She held out the cage.

Billy looked down. The cat shifted a bit in his arms. It pulled open one crusty lid and looked up at him.

The eye gleamed like a dark drop of honey.

Billy got to thinking. His bedroom was quite separate from the rest of the apartment. It was stuck down the hall behind the kitchen on the far side of an old air shaft and the utility room. His dad and mom never went past there. And Billy always kept his door closed.

He shook his head at the woman behind the counter. 'I've changed my mind,' he said.

Maybe he would keep the cat.

TWO

She was a female cat.

Billy hid her around the back of his apartment block in the box of sand saved for winter ice. He went up the back steps of the three-storey building to his apartment. It was on the top floor. His mom and dad were out so he decided to bring the cat inside.

His bedroom wardrobe sat diagonally to the wall. Billy stripped off his jumper and spread it over the floor in the space behind the wardrobe. When he dumped the cat on top, she crumpled into a dark heap and started to shake.

What now?

Her paw dripped steadily. Billy went to the bathroom where his mom kept the first-aid kit. Somewhere in the kit was a cream for skin scrapes. Once he'd found it, he fetched a dish from the kitchen and filled it with warm soapy water. Then he wormed his way to the back of the wardrobe.

When he picked the cat up, she sagged through his fingers like a hank of drain hair. 'Cat,' he said. 'Your paw's festering. It needs attention.'

Billy dunked the bad paw into the warm soapy water and swished it around. He was careful. The cat had claws. He didn't want to be a scratching post. After the paw was well soaked, he cleaned the pus away with a tissue. Somewhere in the process, the cat roused herself and took over. She licked the wound until Billy could see the rawness. When he put on the cream, she shook her paw in the air.

Billy went back downstairs with a foil dish and filled it with sand from the bin. He took it up to his room and shoved it in the space behind his wardrobe. He filled a bowl with fresh cold water and coaxed the cat till it got her attention. She lapped and lapped until the bowl was dry. Billy stayed there while she settled into sleep. Maybe he had a nap too. It didn't seem more than a minute or two before his mom got home.

'Billy!' she called from the hall. 'You haven't touched the meatloaf. Come out of that room and have your dinner.'

'Cat,' Billy warned. 'You'd better be quiet.'

As if he needed to say that. The cat was sleeping

so hard, she was dead to the world.

Billy wiped the black dust away from his arms and face and grabbed another shirt. He turned and surveyed his room. No one would think he was hiding a cat. His room was so messy he could have hidden a pride of lions in there.

After dinner, Billy went back to his bedroom with a chunk of meatloaf in his pocket. He took a glass of milk, too. 'First time I ever saw you take some milk without an argument,' his mom said.

The cat stayed behind the wardrobe for six days. She was as quiet as a wintry night. Sometimes her body shook and Billy had to rest his hand on her back to stop the trembling. When he went to school, he covered her with his dressing gown so she stayed warm. The cat drank lots of water. She ate the food that Billy filched from his dinner plate, and she used the sand litter tray. Every day she licked her injury. When she was done licking, Billy put on the cream. Then she shook her paw.

After a few days, Billy found himself thinking about the cat when he should have been thinking about his science or his maths. Was she warm enough? Did he leave his bedroom door shut? The school days dragged like a loose pair of trousers. After the bell, when all his mates went to the shops, he hurried home. By the time he got to the apartment, he was almost running. He didn't calm down till he looked behind his wardrobe and felt warm breath.

'Cat,' he said. 'I don't want you to die.'

On the seventh day, the cat got up.

Billy was re-lacing his trainers when she peeked around the wardrobe. She wasn't hungry and she didn't need to use the litter. Billy pretended not to notice as she zigzagged her way up close enough to grab a whiff of his socks. They must have smelt all right because she settled down between his feet.

Billy didn't move. His big toe itched but he kept it still.

The cat was all business. First, she lathered her good right paw with spit and burnished her rose-petal nose. She scrubbed her ear inside and out, and smoothed the top of her head. She wiped the crusty bits from her eye. Then she wet her left back paw and washed the other side of her face. With her tongue, she slicked her shoulders, her legs, under her tail, her flanks. She saved the bib beneath her chin for last. By the time she was done grooming, the white patch glowed like a summer cloud.

Finally she stood up. Her eyes gave Billy a look hotter than honey mustard. *Well*, she seemed to say. *What do you think?*

Billy was star-struck.

Was it the same cat? The layers of soot were

gone. Shiny splashes of ink decorated her bronze pelt. There were black rings around her legs and tail. And it could have been his mother's best lace collar tucked under her chin.

She wasn't a grimy stray any more. She was some kind of African queen.

'Cat,' Billy whispered. He reached over and touched one pink ear. 'You should open a beauty parlour.'

He stopped lacing his shoes and rummaged in the cupboard until he found a box. He dumped out the contents and lined the box with a sweat-shirt, a big soft one with a hood. 'You need a new bed,' he said. 'My dad got this top for me in the city. That's a panther on the back.'

The cat inspected Billy's efforts. She jumped in the box and rubbed the folds with her whiskers. She scratched at the sleeves, and chewed the label loose. When the sweatshirt was arranged to her satisfaction, she curled into a crease and closed her eyes.

Billy watched her for a long time.

After supper, Billy emptied his money jar. He went to the pet supply shop on High Street. 'I've got a cat,' he told the lady in the store. 'I need litter and some food. What can I buy for under six dollars?'

A girl stacking shelves was watching him. Billy turned away from her glittery eyes.

The lady took down the cheapest box of kibble and a bag of cat litter. She watched Billy count out his small change. He had just enough. 'What's your name?' she asked.

'Billy,' he answered. 'Billy Reddick.'

'Well, here you go, Billy,' she said, holding out a tin. 'There's a special today. One can of premium food with every purchase.'

After Billy left, the girl stacking jars of fish flakes rolled her eyes. She tossed her silver hoops. 'Joxie,' she scoffed, 'you'll never get rich if you give your stuff away.'

'Now, Salome Davies,' the shop lady said to her assistant, 'don't you be giving me lectures. You belong to the richest family in town. Money never made your grandmother happy and it doesn't make you happy either. That's why the two of you get along so well. You both have other reasons for joy. Trouble is *you* haven't figured yours out yet.'

Salome rolled her glittery eyes.

Billy liked having the cat in his room. The cat liked it too. Or at least he thought she did. Night-times were the best. His bedroom overlooked the back garden of the apartment block. Every night after his mom and dad went to sleep, Billy shoved up the window and sat on the wide sill. He held the cat in his lap. Together they watched the moon polish the branches of the old poplars. They listened to the new leaves talking.

For a few nights, the cat perched stiffly in Billy's arms. She wasn't all that sure about fresh air. Then one evening, she made herself at home. Her bronze coat spread over Billy's lap richer than a royal robe. She dangled her fancy tail off the edge of the sill and let the evening breezes comb the tip. She started to purr.

The first time Billy heard the throaty rattle, he didn't know what it was. He thought someone had switched on a fan. 'Cat,' he whispered, once he had sorted things out. 'You've got a nice motor. But I hope that's all the noise you know how to make. If my dad catches you in my room, it means trouble. He doesn't like cats. *Nobody* in this town likes cats. You guys have too many brothers and sisters, and too many uncles and aunts. You don't respect property rights. You party all night long. Why, the cat-fearing lady next door says you can steal a baby's breath.'

The cat chewed Billy's pyjama button.

'Cat,' Billy said. 'I remember when my mom and dad used to talk instead of yell. One summer we all went down to the river on a fishing trip. My dad showed me how to build a boat out of wood. We sailed that boat right down to the bridge by the old mill. My mom brought a picnic lunch along that day. There was potato salad. She peeled the potatoes herself.'

The cat took a swipe at a passing moth.

'Cat,' Billy said. He stroked her white bib. 'Cat, who threw you away?'

THREE

Salome Davies slipped out of her bedroom window. She climbed down the trumpet vine and ran across the estate lawn. Anybody on High Street looking through the fence towards the posh house wouldn't see the girl. Her clothes were dark. A black cap covered her silver hoop earrings. Anybody looking wouldn't see more than a draught of night air.

Salome was in a hurry. Her grandmother had stayed up late, full of conversation, and she couldn't steal away. Now the night was half over. She darted through the gate by the far edge of the rose garden.

A row of streetlights cast a weak glow across the pavement. High Street looked deserted but Salome wasn't taking any chances. She ducked into the alley along the side of the hardware store.

The store looked much the same as all the other two-storey buildings on High Street. Every one of them had upstairs rooms. Salome grabbed the first rung of the fire escape near the back of the alley and climbed silently past the first-floor flat.

'Cripes,' she cursed. The tenant who lived above the hardware shop had his lights on late. He was always building something. She timed her steps past his landing to match the light knock of his hammer. Once she was on the flat roof, she began to jog across the rooftops, weaving through a jungle of air conditioners and antennae, and circling the odd chimney. At each alley she upped her pace and jumped the gap.

She was as sure-footed as any cat.

When she reached the alley next to Billy's three-storey apartment block, Salome stopped. The building across the way loomed above her. There was no way to jump up the extra storey to the roof.

Her toes inched beyond their perch on the roof edge. Lifting her arms, she pushed her palms flat against the night air and straightened her spine. She focused on the fire escape zigzagging up the side of the apartment block. Then she tipped into space.

Her body did the bridge work.

As soon as her fingers latched on to the diagonal struts of the fire-escape rail across the alley, Salome swung her body through the breach. Her feet hit the bottom of the rail hard, and for a moment her back bowed outwards like a sail in the breeze, her hands and feet pressing into the cold metal. Finally she jumped lightly to the landing. After that, it was an easy climb up the iron stairs to the roof of the apartment building.

From the top, Salome could see the town in all directions. Only the small dome of City Hall down the street and the boarded bell tower of the chapel blocked her view. She walked to the back edge of the apartment roof for a look at the garden, but when she stuck out her head, she got quite a start. A boy sat in a window right under her nose with a cat in his lap. The boy was so close he and Salome could have had a conversation.

Billy didn't know that Salome was looking down on him. He didn't hear anything. And his cat wasn't telling. Both of them were too interested in the drama down in the apartment garden.

The grey tom hunched under the lilac bush.

'Must be a tasty prey,' Billy whispered to his cat. 'It's put that tom under a spell.'

The tom's blue eyes narrowed away from the light of the moon. His ears scoped the quiet. A tiny shuffle in the grass was drawing all his attention. Slowly he began to creep forward, scraping his lean haunches over the wet grass. When the vole broke cover and skittered for a drainpipe, he let rip.

'The mouse's gonna make it!' Billy whispered.

Three metres up, Salome rolled her eyes. The kid was so wrong.

The tom honed in on its prey. His paws skimmed over the earth. When the vole swerved, the cat swerved, as if they were hitched to the same string. Centimetres from the drain, the cat pounced. When he slammed to a stop, his claws were full of felted flesh.

'Wow!' Billy breathed. 'That's one good hunter!'

The cat on Billy's lap sunk her claws into his pyjamas. Her amber eyes glittered. She knew more than Billy did.

Salome smirked. At least that kid had got something right. She backed away from the edge of the roof and returned to running rooftops. At the alley next to the chapel, she grabbed a thick mulberry branch and swung on to the shingles of the little church. When the tom came home, she was waiting.

The tom ignored the girl on the roof. He jumped down from the wooden fence into the chapel yard with his trophy. Gently he placed the limp carcass on the table of brown earth. He organized the tiny limbs, pushing them into place, prodding the soft body into a pretty mound. Then he began to eat. He ate from one end to the other, as if the vole were a stick of liquorice. The tail made a lip-smacking finish.

Salome saluted the tom from her perch on the chapel roof before crawling under a loose board in the bell tower. She had her own game inside the church so it wasn't long before the stained glass above the chapel door began to glow. Lucky none of the people out late at night on High Street noticed the rosy blush above their heads. People out at that time had better things to think about.

Besides, the bell in the tower was long gone.

Nobody in Clydesdale looked up any more.

FOUR

Billy's folks didn't suspect he had a cat.

His room was leftover space. Nobody else used the hall past the utility room. When his mom wanted Billy, she yelled from the kitchen. And if his dad wanted something, it didn't matter where he was. He yelled right there.

Billy was a smart boy. He did his best to keep the cat a secret.

Cat hair was a problem – it seemed to stick to his clothes until he was more cat than boy. When the time looked right, Billy said to his mom, 'I'm old enough to go to the launderette on my own. Can I have some change for the machines?' Billy was careful with the litter tray, too. Every morning he wrapped the used litter in plastic and carted it away in his school bag. And he stuck to his old habits. He tried not to run to his room when he came home from school. He left some supper on his plate, and pinched it later when no one was looking. And he kept his room the way he always kept it.

Messy.

Billy and the cat had more fun than a barrel of monkeys in all the clutter. Billy made up games. He tied an eraser to a string. When he dragged the toy between his shoes, the cat skittered after it. She pounced on the soft rubber. At other times he stalked the cat through the legs of his bed. He poked the rings on her tail, or the spots on her back.

If Billy forgot to watch out, the cat got even. She ambushed his hand. Or she untied his shoelaces.

One day he made a paper aeroplane and flew it across the room. The cat brought it back and dropped it at his feet. Billy was so impressed that he got down on the floor to thank her properly. 'Good girl,' he said. He ran his fingers over her bronze coat and let her backbone cup his hand. Then he threw the aeroplane again. By the time the game was over, the plane was a damp ball of crumpled paper. 'Cat,' Billy said. He lay down on the floor so they were eye to eye. 'Cat, do you think you're a dog?'

When Billy went to school, the cat explored his room. She got into the seat of Billy's jeans, and hid in the drawers of the wardrobe. One day he found her peeking out of a rubber rain boot. There was nothing she couldn't get inside.

Nothing but his lunchbox.

That lunchbox put the cat in a snit. It was made of tin, with a latch that slipped sideways. Whenever Billy left the box in his room, the cat turned it into homework. She could have written a test, she studied it so much. One day when Billy took out his maths sums, the smell of his leftover tuna sandwich drove her crazy. She scraped her cheek along the side of the pail and tapped the latch with her paws. She scratched at the corners. Then she crouched down low and glared at the box with her butt up. She stayed that way for a long time.

Maybe she thought the lunchbox would sprout legs and take off.

Billy worked on a maths problem. *If Mark had two and a quarter bars of chocolate and Kristen ate two thirds, how much does Mark have left?*

As far as Billy was concerned, Kristen had eaten more than her share. That was all anyone needed to know. He put down his pencil. 'Here, cat,' he said. 'I'll show you how it works.' He pushed the latch of the lunchbox sideways and swung open the top. He even offered her a bit of the old bread crust before he snapped the lid shut and got back to the maths question.

The cat ignored the food. She kept watching

the box. Finally she walked over and tipped it sideways. She tormented the latch with her paw. When that didn't work, she shoved the box against the bed leg and pawed it some more. The next time Billy looked at her, she was sitting right in the box with a tuna crust in her mouth.

Billy pulled the cat on to his lap and watched her clean her paws. Her spit smelt like fish. 'You're one smart cat,' he said. 'If you were a human, you could do my maths homework. Anybody as smart as you needs a proper name.'

Billy had never named anything before. And the cat was special. She knew how to be quiet. She cleaned up after herself. And she liked his conversation. He had to think of a name that said all those things. 'How about Dot?' he offered.

The cat slewed her golden eyes sideways. She climbed out of his lap. Her tail flicked the air.

Nope.

'Mabel?' Billy asked.

The cat closed her eyes and arched her ink-splattered back. She didn't want a name for a smart cat. She didn't want a name for a cat with manners.

Billy rubbed the hollow between her shoulder blades. He got down and grinned. 'How about "Skinny Bones"?' he teased.

Humph! She didn't rattle and clatter. She wasn't a stack of sticks.

She slipped under the wardrobe.

Billy wracked his brains. He remembered the old comics in the wire rack at the newsagent. There was one called *Conga, the Empress of Zar*. On the cover the Empress sat on a throne among her sons. She was dressed in a copper dress with splotches of black. A baby slept in her lap. There were leopards at her feet.

It was a good comic even if it was old. Billy had read the whole thing, standing there while the little Chinese lady watched him from behind the counter. The Empress had inherited her empire as a girl. She and her people were forced into hiding by a raiding tribe. When she returned to reclaim her land, she led an army of wild cats ridden by her four young sons. They drove out the trespassers. From then on, the empire of Zar became strong and secret. It flourished away from predatory eyes. And no one ever found it again.

Billy crawled under the wardrobe. The cat regarded him with eyes full of heavy syrup. 'Hey,' Billy said. 'How about I call you Conga?'

The cat poured out of her bed box. She rubbed her cheek against Billy's ear. Her paw mussed his hair. Then she jumped to the windowsill so the sunset could set her pelt afire.

Conga.

She liked it.

FIVE

That night Billy and Conga had ringside seats to a brawl.

They were sitting on the windowsill watching the back garden when some eyes showed up. They hovered in the lilac shadows, green and blue flashlights, black-slitted, unblinking.

Up in Billy's window, Conga tensed. Her tail swung as hard as a bug swatter. When Billy pulled her close, her whiskers pricked his chin.

Ssss...t! The eyes disappeared. Moments later, two cats sprang to the rim of the fence. They were pumped up, ragged as haystacks.

Get out! one squalled. *This is my yard!*

Oroww! the other yowled back. *Make me!*

The toms were spoiling for a fight, their tails crooked like crowbars. They spat. They growled. Then they began screaming. When one held up a fist full of nails, they ran at each other. Scraps of fur flew into the eyes of the moon.

Billy held Conga firmly. 'Stop that,' he whispered harshly at the whirling mess of claws and tails. 'Stop, you two!'

The warning came too late. The kitchen light went on. Boots thundered on to the landing of the fire escape outside, close to Billy's window. His dad was up!

Billy grabbed Conga and ducked back into his room so fast he knocked his noggin on the frame. He pressed his back against the wall. Conga squirmed in his arms, but he gripped her close to his chest. Below him the backyard wailed like a roomful of hungry babies.

His dad leant over the railing. 'Shaddup, you mangy flea-bitten devils!' he cursed angrily. 'Get outta here!'

Billy dared a sideways glance out of the window. A boot gyrated though the air and hit the ground with a soft thud. When its mate slammed into the fence, the yard emptied. One of the cats dropped over into the next yard. The other drew a streak of silver across the grass.

It was the grey tom.

'Those cats are dead meat,' Billy's dad muttered. He switched off the light and slammed the kitchen door behind him. Billy could hear him clomping back to bed.

'Conga, we've gotta watch out,' he whispered. 'That's my dad and he's talking about *you*.' He carried his cat behind the wardrobe and stroked her neck hairs until they settled smooth and shining. Then he crawled into bed.

So did Conga.

When Billy woke up, she was draped over his head, all her engines going. One soft paw plugged his nose. A tail tickled his throat.

Billy didn't move.

He just lay there wearing his cat as a hat.

SIX

Billy's father, Walter Reddick, woke up in a foul mood. The catfight had spoiled his sleep. And worse luck, he needed his boots. He dragged a red checked jacket over his old jogging suit and wrenched open the door to the landing. It was three flights of stairs to the back garden and he tromped down every one of them.

'Blasted cats,' he swore. 'I should have thrown a can of beans.' He retrieved one of his boots from under the lilac bush. There was no sign of the other. It was probably over the fence in the supermarket car park.

Reddick strung out a clothesline of cuss words. All the backyards in the street had the same high fences. He'd have to go out to High Street and hike down the alley behind the Lebanese restaurant where the fence had a board missing. What a waste of time!

Reddick ploughed down the apartment alley. He was so mad he almost ran into the ponytailed kid, who was rooting through the rubbish bins. He didn't give the boy a second glance. One of those street kids, he thought. Didn't look but five years older than his own Billy, and already a drain on society.

Reddick pulled his coat collar around his ears and kicked an empty lemonade bottle. Behind the Lebanese restaurant, he pushed through the space in the fence and came out on Haven Street. He turned back towards the supermarket. The car park was empty. His boot lay among the weeds at the far end of it, close up to the boards. Reddick retrieved it angrily.

He hoped it had walloped the cats.

He looked over the fence at his apartment. His wife was watching him from their third-storey window. Reddick ignored her. He retraced his steps down the street and through the alley between the shops so fast that he almost ran into the tom skimming alongside the brick. The cat gave him a frosty stare before squeezing under the fence.

That icy glance really got Reddick going. By the time he reached the front door of the apartment building, his temper was bigger than he was. He lumbered up the stairs, and shoved open the door to the apartment.

Billy was at the kitchen table eating cereal. His mother was making coffee.

'It's Billy's birthday,' Mae said, looking at her husband carefully. There was a present on the table. It was a book.

'As if I don't know it's my own kid's birthday,' he griped. He tossed his boots in the corner and slung his jacket after them. 'Time you stopped filling his head with fairy tales. I've got him a real birthday present.' He fetched a long parcel from the bedroom and slammed it over the book. 'Now look here, Billy. You're underage. But the law don't need to know about that. We'll just get in a bit of practice ahead of time. Won't be long after that till you're hunting with your old man.'

Billy's mom came over to the table. She eyed the package warily. 'He's only eleven, Walter. I don't want him to have that now.'

'Quit your fretting, Mae. The boy's practically grown. That thing will keep down the vermin. Now you go on, Billy, and open the package.'

Billy tore off the paper and looked at the gun.

His dad crossed his arms. 'You know what that is, boy. I showed you before. That's an air rifle, and it's a good one – high velocity. I paid top dollar for it. Shoots real silver pellets. It'll take out a crow if you aim it right. We'll go out for a drive some day, you and me. Give you a chance to practise. I didn't put a bullet in that deer's heart with no practice.'

Reddick thumbed the air.

Billy followed his dad's gesture to the stag head mounted on the wall. The eyes seemed to stare back at Billy as if the whole thing was his fault.

Reddick paused. He was thinking about the grey tom. Once the idea caught up to his mouth, he grinned. 'Come to think of it, I know a critter that's volunteering to be a target. We'll wait till the time's right.' He put up his arms and pretended to shoot.

Billy picked up the rifle. It looked like the real thing, long, heavy, the dark barrel gleaming with fresh oil. His mom was staring at it. His dad was staring at him. Billy didn't know what to say. But he had to say something.

Finally he got it out. 'Thanks, Dad. It's a great present. But I'd better get ready for school now.'

It was lame and he knew it, but it was the best he could muster. He ran to the toilet and turned on the tap. The fighting started as soon as he got the door closed.

What else was new? His mom and dad were always at each other. Only this time they were fighting over his birthday present. Even with the door shut, Billy could hear the shouting. His dad's voice made the lock rattle. 'I'm doing Billy a favour, you hear me. He'd be a sissy-boy if you had your way. A wimp! Once he's learned how to hunt, he'll grow up – be a man.'

Billy wondered how long the argument would last. He turned up the tap so he could think. Maybe his dad was right. A gun like that – he bet none of his friends had a gun like that.

He came out of the toilet. 'I forgot,' he said. 'I need to buy a scrapbook for school. The five and ten store will be open. Mom, where are all the markers?'

That put a stop to the shouting for a bit. His mom rummaged in the kitchen drawers. His dad slugged back his coffee. 'Sure, kid. Stick that gun in the back of your cupboard. Keep your mouth shut for now. And don't go touching it until I teach you the ropes. We wouldn't want to scare your mother.'

The kitchen drawer crashed into the counter.

Billy fled to his room.

Reddick grabbed his toolbox and slammed out of the kitchen door. Blasted cats. He'd like to throttle every last one of 'em.

SEVEN

Conga was getting bigger. It wasn't just the food. Her tummy was swelling up like a bag of chestnuts. The first day of the summer holidays, Billy worked it out.

She was going to have babies.

Billy flung himself on to the bed. It was all too much. He'd never be able to keep that a secret. Besides he didn't know anything about how to take care of a cat full of kittens.

Sometimes, it seemed like nothing ever went right.

Conga jumped up on the bed and stole between his arms. She kneaded his neck and purred in his ear. Her rough tongue scraped his nose. 'Okay, okay,' Billy said, rolling over. 'I'm here.' He traced one of her leopard spots. 'But if you're growing little ones, I've got to make some money. You'll need to eat right.'

Billy took a sorry look in his money jar. He wasn't much of a saver. Most of the time the jar emptied out as fast as the coins hit the bottom. It took some thinking before he decided to collect bottles and return them for the deposit. Corky's, the five and ten store, had started recycling and refilling them. He decided to start right away.

The thinking turned out to be easier than the doing. For a few days, Billy searched up and down High Street, and into the side roads. Someone always got to the bins before he did. And worse luck, one of the girls from school saw him swiping a whisky bottle from an alley.

His face burned. He could hear her now, calling across the street for the whole town to hear. 'Hey, Billeeee, are you a garbage picker or somethin'?'

After that, Billy got up early so he didn't have to duck his mates when he checked out the garbage. Most of them slept late. And the pickings in the alley bins were better anyway. The only other competition out at that time of day was the older kid with the ponytail.

One morning Billy and the bigger boy both ended up pawing in the same bin. Billy hurried to grab all the loose bottles. The other guy picked out some broken glass.

What did that guy want with a piece of pink plate?

As Billy was turning to leave, the kid spoke up. 'Hey,' he said to Billy. 'There's a whole case of beer bottles at the bottom. You missed 'em.'

Billy was surprised. He smiled at the bigger boy. 'Thanks,' he said.

His money jar began to gain weight. Billy took the beer bottles and the fizzy-drink bottles back to Corky's. When his dad gave him money for drinks, he pocketed the change and drank water. A boy at school gave him five bucks for his old soccer shoes, and he got ten dollars for helping a family catch their budgie. After a week he had a stash of cash.

'I need some good food,' he said to the lady at the pet store. 'My cat's going to have babies.'

'When's the big day?' the lady asked.

Billy thought about it. 'I don't know. Maybe she's been growing her kits for a month or more.'

'You've got about five weeks to wait then, give or take,' the lady said.

Billy was looking at cat toys when the pony-tailed kid walked into the store.

'How's it going, Luke?' the pet store lady asked.

The boy slung his backpack on the counter. 'I need another bag of kibble, Joxie,' he said. 'Make it a big one. And a couple of cans of fish for the cat that's ailing.'

The boy was wearing his City Hall shirt. Billy moved a little closer.

'Think I'll give the chapel yard a good sweep tonight,' Luke went on.

'Spring cleaning for cats,' Joxie snorted. She handed him a can of food. 'You should get yourself a girlfriend, Luke. How old are you? Maybe seventeen and that's a stretch. Now that you make a living from City Hall, it's time you stopped spending every last dollar on those cats.'

Luke waved goodbye. 'You should talk,' he said as he went out the door.

As soon as he was gone, the pet store lady called down the aisle to her assistant, the girl that made Billy nervous, the one with the glittery eyes. 'Salome, that Luke is a nice young man. How come you get scarce every time he's in the store? You two ought to strike up an acquaintance. It would give you something else to do besides wander where you're not wanted.'

'I've got no time for boyfriends,' Salome growled. When she caught Billy looking, she gave him a stare that could torch stone.

Billy paid for the food and hurried out of the shop. The boy named Luke was heading down High Street away from the chapel. That suited Billy. Luke had talked about cats in the church-yard. Billy was going to see for himself.

Maybe one of those chapel cats already knew Conga. Maybe one of them was going to be a daddy.

EIGHT

The narrow alley made Billy nervous. But behind the chapel was a surprise, a lovely yard, hot and sunny and quiet. A ramshackle castle of crates and boards and wooden barrels leaned up against the fence. At the back there was an old stable with a collapsed roof, and he could just make out two stalls where someone had once kept a pair of horses. Leaning against the partition was a piece of wagon wheel, and there was an old manger nailed to the back wall.

Billy couldn't see any cats but he knew enough to keep looking. Cats were good at camouflage. Why, his Conga was so quiet, she could hide in plain sight. At last he picked out a grey button nose poking from an old planter. He spotted a lick of ear between some planks. And there was a powder-puff cheek twitching inside a tub.

'Hey! What are *you* doing here?'

Billy whipped about. Luke had come around the back of the sheds. He had ditched his City Hall shirt. His backpack weighed down his shoulder.

'My name's Billy Reddick,' Billy said. 'I'm looking at the cats.'

The older boy gave him a close look. 'You like cats?' he grunted. He sounded suspicious.

'I like 'em fine.' Billy said. 'I've got one of my own. She's going to have babies.'

'There are enough babies already,' the boy retorted. But he looked relieved. He put down his kit and took out the bag of kibble. 'I saw you in the pet store,' he went on. 'So you already know my name is Luke – Luke Malone. And if you want to see cats, you came to the right place. The show's about to start.'

They stood waiting together in the sunshine.

The cats roused themselves little by little. Little by little, they poked out their brown noses, their pink ones, their black ears and orange ears and vanilla-dipped ears, their wire whiskers. Things began to work, eyes opening, muscles stretching, tongues lapping, paws scrubbing. And tails – the tails lifted. They swayed like silk ropes in the lazy air.

Little by little, the cats came out of their rickety hidey-holes. They yawned. They stretched. They greeted one another, butting heads, kissing cheeks, rubbing up against the rough boards. The grey tom lifted his wide head lazily from the highest crate, his eyes half closed. One paw stuck through a knot hole, testing the weather. When Luke got out the food, the cat sprung to a fence post and fixed his cold gaze on the bag.

'That grey one is the king of the castle,' Luke said. 'And those three mackerels over there, those are the copycats.'

Billy followed Luke's gaze. Three cats, each exactly like the next, paraded into the centre of the yard. They had stripes of black and silver, and whitewashed feet. Their tails swished back and forth as steady as clockwork. Billy watched them circle in towards the food. When the first one stopped, the others did the same. They sat in a neat line and *row rowed* for dinner.

'One can't even pee without the other two doing the same,' Luke muttered.

A bit of dirty scruff stuck its head out of a box. *Feed me*, it yawrled. *Hurry!* It scratched at the stable wall.

'That cat is the beggar of the group,' Luke said. 'Answers to the name of Scat. Eats like a pig and never gets any bigger. It's so prickly, all the other cats keep their distance.'

More cats appeared. Two gingery toms eased from a stable rafter as smoothly as thick drips of oil. They had heavy fur and big paws. A white cat crawled out from a turned-over clay plant pot, and another one, a patchwork of red, white and cream, dropped from a tree limb. The last cat to show up was all black. It slunk into the middle of the yard with its eyes shut.

'What's wrong with that one?' Billy asked.

'Blind,' Luke said. 'It's been that way ever since I took over the care of the colony. Probably scuffled with another cat. Or maybe a badger got at it. Its roaming days are over.'

Luke put dry food in the cups and plates scattered over the yard. The water pan was almost dry. He topped it with cool water from his thermos. 'Teatime,' he called.

All the cats reacted. Invisible magnets yanked Scat's fur every which way as the little cat sprang for a chipped cup of kibble. The grey tom stepped up next, taking his time. He crouched and began to eat, chewing a pellet, intent on the pleasure of the crack against his teeth. The other cats gathered around the last pile. All their heads dipped into the same pool.

A weak cry came from inside the stable ruins. Billy went over and peered in the manger. The thing buried in some blanket scraps hardly looked like a cat. Half the hair was gone. One leg didn't sit right. And it had a missing ear.

'That cat's on the way out,' Luke said. 'Food is about the only thing left for it to enjoy.' He emptied a tin of fish on to a piece of crockery inside the manger, and added water to a tin clipped to the side.

The cat struggled to its feet. When Billy reached out to move the dish closer, Luke knocked his arm away. 'Are you crazy?' he said. 'These cats are wild. That feral could still take a chunk of your hand. Just hang on. It'll eat when it finds the time.'

'It looks pretty bad,' Billy said. 'Why don't you take it to a vet?' He watched as the sick cat squatted next to the food.

Luke snorted. 'Who's got that kind of money? Might as well buy a piece of the moon.'

'How come you're feeding the cats?' Billy asked. 'Where are all the owners?'

'Some of 'em never had one,' grunted Luke. 'Others weren't so lucky. I found the three mack-erels tossed in a bin. They were all of six weeks. And the white one . . . someone ditched her in that big snow last winter. Scat came in with a burnt-out firecracker tied to its tail. I don't know about the rest. They were already here. The guy who used to tend them has gone now.'

Billy watched the cat in the manger. The first time he had seen Conga on the street, she was half dead too. Now she was so full of life, she was making more of the stuff.

Suddenly Billy needed to make sure his cat was okay. 'I've gotta go,' he said.

Luke grabbed Billy's arm as he made for the alley. 'Just keep this place to yourself, okay? The town's not friendly. A lot of folk bear the cats a grudge. No need to stoke the fire.'

Billy nodded.

He knew all about keeping his mouth shut.

NINE

In a cat-hating town, the ferals do their business after the sun sets.

The three silver-striped mackerels jumped from the crates to the back fence. One after the other, they left the chapel yard and pawed into new land. They scouted the freshly planted back gardens until they found one to their liking. The first cat sprayed scent over the porch and the new lawn chair. The second scratched at the willow sapling. The last tabby rubbed against the plant pot and squatted on the tender buds.

Then they lined up on the fence in a pretty row and crooned to the moon.

Mr Thomas turned over in bed. 'Those cats need a tune-up,' he complained to his wife.

The blind cat ventured down the chapel alley. It tasted the wet night air and felt the tap of a grasshopper. It smelt the bitter dandelion. Still in the shelter of the close walls, it listened to the soft swoosh of a late-night car rolling down High Street.

A couple out for a midnight stroll walked along the pavement with their big dog. 'Take the leash off the dog for a bit,' the girl sweet-talked her boyfriend. 'It's late. No one will see. The dog wants to run.'

The blind cat didn't expect a silly dog to scramble into the alley. When the dog started to bark, the noise echoed off the bins. The vibrations confounded the cat and sent it scrabbling the wrong way into the street. It careened across the road straight into a brick wall.

The girl laughed. 'Come here, boy!' she called out to the dog. 'Did you scare that cat? What a brave doggy!'

Across the street, the blind cat leant close to a strange wall.

Which way was home?

The grey tom went hunting for a mouse meal.

Billy's father heard yowling in his dreams. He staggered out to the kitchen and peeled back a can of beer. 'I gotta get that cat,' he muttered. He went out and leant over the landing. He didn't see the grey tom waiting under the lilac bush. He didn't see Billy and Conga either.

Those two were pressed up to the plaster next to Billy's bedroom window.

When the sun woke up, the street cats headed for their nests while the people crawled out of their beds. Salome climbed up her grandmother's vine as the sun's rays caught the greenery. Half in, half out of the window, she held her breath. The house was quiet. She tumbled the rest of the way into her bedroom and pushed a button on the phone. 'Salome Davies,' she said, after the machine picked up. She steadied her breathing. 'Officer Jean, I'm checking in.'

An hour later, Officer Jean listened to the morning messages. She made a record of Salome's call. Then she read over Salome's rap sheet.

Name: **Salome Davies**
Age: Fourteen

Apprehended: 06/15/2008
    Unlawful entry of restaurant
    (Found in kitchen, sniffing contents of spice rack)

Plea Entered: Guilty

Apprehended: 09/19/2008
> Unlawful entry of public property
> (Found in museum storage room after closure, drawing dinosaur bones)

Plea Entered: Guilty

Apprehended: 12/03/2009
> Unlawful entry of commercial residence
> (Found in hotel attic, hanging Christmas ornaments on rafters)

Plea Entered: Guilty

Officer Jean sighed. There was a string of infractions in the report. Before a judge, Salome had pleaded curiosity. 'I like to know about stuff,' she had told him. 'I never take anything.'

At her fourth court appearance, the judge had lost his temper. 'That's not the point,' he had ranted. 'You can't go wherever you want. It's trespassing. You have the makings of a cat burglar. The court should tie a bell around your neck.'

Salome's grandmother had spoken up. 'I live in Clydesdale,' she had said to the judge. 'It's a quiet town in the country. Salome can volunteer at the local pet store. I'll make sure she stays put at night. Her parents need a break.'

The judge had agreed. 'Make sure that girl

follows the rules. She has to check in with the youth officer from home first thing every morning and last thing at night. Next time she stands in front of me, I'll throw the book at her.'

Officer Jean closed Salome's file and went back to her messages. It was so far, so good. Salome checked in every day, right as rain.

It looked like the girl was cured.

At seven in the morning, Luke fed the cats. When the blind one didn't come out for breakfast, he started looking. He looked for the cat for so long, he was late for work at City Hall.

Salome had breakfast with her grandmother in the dining room. They had crumpets with marmalade on white bone china, and orange juice served with mint leaves in the Hartford crystal. 'Those drawings you stuck on the fridge are quite good,' Mrs Davies was saying. 'We'll have to see about lessons. You've got a talent, Salome. But you need some direction – and lots of practice.'

Salome smiled. She liked her grandmother. 'Got to go,' she said. 'Joxie's expecting me down at the pet store.'

Her grandmother watched her leave. Her parents have raised her fine, she thought. Those wild roaming days were just a phase. The girl had settled down.

* * *

Down the street and over the fence, Mr Thomas went from his bed to his garden. As soon as the old man got a whiff of cat piss, he called Animal Services. 'Last night, some cats fouled my garden,' he griped. 'They scratched the willow and tore up my flowerbeds. The buds in the planter are as hard as dried peas. I bet they came from the cat colony out by the pizza parlour on Weston Road. Somebody's got to see to those cats.'

After he hung up, the little apricot kitten rubbed against his leg. It mewed softly.

'Does Wiggins want his milk?' Mr Thomas asked. He picked up his kitty and went to the fridge.

Animal Services sent a man and a truck over to the cat colony on Weston Road. The ferals scattered as soon as they heard the motor. The man tore down the shelters and cut back the bushes. He raked the ground and sprayed the soil. Later, when the cats crept back, their shelters were gone. Only thing left behind was an eviction notice.

The Animal Services man made one more stop on the way back to the garage. He scraped a dead black cat off the street. 'Somebody got their luck back,' he joked to himself. He didn't really think the joke was funny. But then working for a living wasn't funny either.

* * *

Billy's dad came home for lunch early. He was in a foul mood. 'I'm taking the rest of the day off,' he announced over his ploughman's lunch. 'Those roofs can wait. The boy and I are going to have some quality time in the country.'

Billy's mom looked up from her books. 'Walter Reddick,' she objected. 'Our son needs to do his laundry today.'

His dad turned to Billy. 'Grab your gear. Your mom's a mite nervous about seeing her boy grow up. All that schooling's got her head twisted round.' He turned back to his wife with his chest puffed up. 'Now, don't you go telling me what's best for the boy, Mae. You can pour me a cold one and make like a good wife. Do what you're told.'

Billy hid in his bedroom while they had it out. When he went back to the kitchen, his mom had gone.

'Time to get started,' said his dad. The air had gone out of his lungs and he sagged against the kitchen chair. 'Go fetch that rifle.'

The man had gotten his way.

But it didn't feel that good.

TEN

Billy sat in the front seat of the truck. He cradled the air rifle in his arms, letting the steel barrel cool his hot skin. It was a handsome piece of work, as long as a metre stick. The walnut stock was satin smooth. Billy traced the knots with his finger.

'That gun's a beauty, all right,' his dad said. 'A Daisy. A gun with class. Pump it to the max and the shot will ring true. The work will put some muscle on those skinny arms of yours.'

They pulled off the road a few miles outside of town. Billy followed his dad down a rough path, holding the gun broke in the middle and angled down the way he'd been shown, until the woods opened into a meadow.

In the high grass, Billy's dad swung around and bent down until they were face to face. 'Now,

Billy,' he said, 'if anyone asks, that's *my* gun. I'm just letting you take a shot. No need to mention the birthday. Law says you gotta be sixteen to own a gun like that. The way I see it, that's waiting too long. You need to get your hunting eye young.'

He paced out fifteen metres and tied a red rag to a sapling. He fit the scope in place on the rifle and adjusted the level, then handed Billy a pellet. 'Put it in, boy,' he declared. 'Let's get this show on the road.'

Billy's hand was clammy. The silver shot felt slick. Clumsily, he set one into the barrel, clicked the gun together and held up the rifle.

'See those cross hair lines,' his dad instructed. 'Line 'em up with the rag before you shoot. Once you feel the recoil, you'll know how to make up for it next time. The rifle's got a great knock-down. You'll be able to hit a squirrel at twenty metres. Blast the cocky varmint right off its perch.'

His dad adjusted the handle steady against Billy's shoulder. Billy found the thin hairs crossed in the scope and moved them until they hovered over the red cloth. He pulled the trigger.

The report was loud. Billy jumped. He stared at the target. The rag hung quietly from the branch.

Billy's dad shook his head. 'You missed, boy! You've got to stay steady. That rifle will try to fight you back. Next time, expect the recoil. Pump 'er up and have another go.' He handed his son a pellet.

Billy pulled at the base of the gun three times. Each time the gun resisted a little more.

'Keep pumping,' his dad ordered. 'The rifle needs to be packed with air. You won't get any distance if you don't pump her up.'

Billy pushed again. The gun locked. Four times.

'Again.'

Billy started to sweat. He pushed. The gun pushed back. He couldn't do it.

'Put some weight into it,' his dad demanded.

Billy shoved with all his might.

The gun locked. Five times.

His dad nodded. 'It'll do seven. You've got to eat more meat and potatoes, if that's the best you can do. Now, this time stay steady. Keep your eye on the crosshairs. Go for the gusto!'

Billy planted his feet apart and raised the gun. Through the scope his target hung like a red flag in a blue sky. This time he braced for the backlash.

And this time the rag whipped up.

'Smokin'!' his dad said. 'That's my boy. You'll be a credit in the field to your old man.' He had Billy shoot for half an hour.

Back in the car, Billy could feel his arm muscles quivering. He held the red rag in his hands. It was full of holes. The rifle sat warm and quiet back in the boot.

'Now, son, this bit o' practice stays between you and me,' his dad was saying. 'I don't want your ma to know the details. She's got some bleeding-heart ideas about animals. The land would be plumb overrun with critters if she had her way. I'm a working man. I don't need to waste time trying to make your mother see the sense of it. We'll leave the gun in the back. I'll take it up later.'

He switched on the radio. The local news was on.

'The mayor has announced that a town forum will be held next week after the council reports,' said the newsreader. 'The debate will discuss the feral cat population. Clydesdale is overrun with wild cats, and resentment against the animals is on the rise. Citizens are divided on ways to deal with the problem. Whatever the outcome, most people want action on the issue sooner rather than later.'

'Ha!' said Billy's dad, slapping him on the leg. 'No good cat 'cept a dead cat. There's only one solution to the cat problem. Guess I'll go to that meeting.'

Billy just sat in his seat thinking. His head was stuffed full of his dad's thoughts. He could hardly find room for his own.

ELEVEN

All July, Conga ate like each meal was her last.
Billy talked to his cat as she ate, and as she
groomed, and even during her naps. He talked to
her at night while they sat in the bedroom
window. Conga always lent him an ear. Only
sometimes she stuck her round honey eyes into
his dark hazel ones. She wanted to make sure Billy
wasn't making up stories.

Between talks, Billy found and returned bottles.
He earned errand money from the neighbours. He
did groceries with his mom, and practised
shooting with his dad. With all the things to do,
there wasn't much time to spend with his mates.
Whenever he did show up at the park or the community centre, they gave him a hard time.

'Getting kind of rare, aren't you?'

'Hey Billy, you got a girlfriend or somethin'?'

One day, Billy paid a visit to the library. He wanted to know what to do when the time came for the kits to be born. When they saw him coming out with a book, his friends jeered. ''S that a good book, Billy? Gee, maybe you could teach me how to read.'

After that, Billy did his research in secret.

Billy helped at the cat colony, too. The white cat was pregnant. Luke cursed when he realized she was growing kits. 'I should have had that cat fixed,' he said. 'I could have found the money somehow.'

Billy attempted a few questions while the older boy shoved insulation around the white cat's plant pot. 'Luke,' he asked, 'what do you do at City Hall?'

Luke wasn't much of a talker. 'I clean,' he said. He cut a piece of plywood with his band saw and added it to a pile. The white cat sat in the shadows watching him anxiously. She wanted to get back inside her home.

'You don't look old enough to work,' Billy said.

'I'm near seventeen. That's legal age.' Luke fit two of the pieces into a v-shaped roof and screwed in some hinges. He was good with his hands.

'Where are your folks?'

'Don't know. We went our separate ways.'

'Where do you live?'

'I've got a room over the hardware store.'

Finally Billy asked the question that was always on his mind. 'Why did you want that pink glass plate?'

Luke looked at Billy as if he had two heads. He got gruff. 'What are you talking about?'

'We looked in the same bin one morning,' Billy said. 'At the apartment block. I took the bottles. But all you wanted was a broken plate. It was pink—'

Luke cut Billy off. 'I've got a project,' he said, hoisting the new roof over the plant pot. 'It's something to help out these cats.' He attached the sides to the slopes with screws. 'There's not much use in telling you. I wrote to the mayor and made a proposal. He never sent me an answer. I guess the mayor and council are too busy for the likes of me.'

A project? What kind of project uses a pink glass plate? Billy changed the subject. 'How come you don't name the cats?'

Luke stuck more straw in the spaces between the cat's pot and the plywood cover. He lined the base of the big pot, too. 'Naming the cats is a waste of time,' he snorted. 'A name means you've got a place in the world. The ferals aren't that lucky. Once the city finds out about this colony, the cats will be driven out of town. Or worse.' He stood up and brushed off the sawdust.

The white cat scurried back inside her pot. They could hear her scratching out a new nest in the straw.

'You call the crazy one Scat,' Billy said stubbornly. 'That's a name.'

'That one needed naming,' Luke retorted. 'It's been a holy terror since it moved into the colony. Now that it's taken over the manger, it thinks it owns the whole yard.'

That was the truth. After the sick cat had died, Scat claimed the manger lock and stock. The little spitfire almost split into parts when any other cat ventured too close.

Billy started to sweep the yard. His silence did the talking.

After a few minutes, Luke relented. 'I suppose you could name 'em,' he said. 'Who knows? Maybe the mayor will take some responsibility. Maybe my project will get off the ground and these cats will get a real home. All I need is a miracle.' He turned to Billy. 'But I haven't heard of none of those around here.'

Billy rested in the shade of the old stable and started to think. There were nine cats in the colony. Besides Scat, he needed eight names. 'We'll call the white one Snowflake,' he said. 'And the snooty orange ones can answer to Mac and Cheese.'

The three silver-striped mackerels poked out

their heads. Billy remembered some names from the family fishing trip. 'Pike, Perch and Pickerel,' he decided.

Luke pointed to the red, black and white cat checking out an ant hole. 'That one is a Nosy Parker,' he said.

'Done,' said Billy.

Only the grey tom was left. Billy was plumb out of ideas. He watched the cat swagger into a leftover patch of sun.

'Leave it,' said Luke. 'The name will come to you.'

When Billy got home, his mom was stretched out on the couch with a textbook on her lap. ''Bout time you got home, young man!' she declared. 'We need to talk. You come with me right now.'

Billy's legs turned to jelly. He bit his lip as he followed his mom around the air shaft, and past the utility room. The door to his room was ajar. And the bedroom window was wide open.

His mom waved her arms. 'Billy, look at this place!' she complained. 'You live like an animal. How do you find anything? Your clothes aren't meant to be carpet cover. There's a cupboard and a wardrobe for that stuff. You get in there and pick up your things. I opened that window to let in some air.' She clomped back down the hall. 'As if I haven't got enough to do with my coursework *and* looking after you and your father.'

Billy closed his bedroom door behind her. His heart was twanging his ribs. It pumped so hard he lost his breath. 'Conga!' he choked. 'Conga, where are you?'

He got down on his knees and looked behind the wardrobe. No cat. He looked under the bed. No cat. He checked the cupboard. Nothing. So he stuck his head out of the open window.

The yard was empty.

Maybe she had run away.

'Conga,' Billy whispered. 'Conga, please be here.' He pulled the sweaters out of the drawers. He dumped the garbage from the bin. He yanked the sheets off the bed. He even checked the inside of his pillows. He was about to take to the back stairs when the sleeve of his dressing gown twitched inside the laundry bag.

Billy swooped down and pulled Conga out of the pile of clothes. He wanted to hug her. He wanted to bury his nose in her fur. Only Conga was in no mood for cuddles. She wriggled out of his arms and jumped to the floor. Her tail slapped his leg. She was madder than a hornet's nest.

Billy let her go. He pulled the window down a little and put the garbage back in the bin. He picked up his things. He straightened his covers. Then he crawled behind the wardrobe and tried to make peace. 'Conga,' he whispered. 'That was my mom. She doesn't mean you any harm. She doesn't even know you're here.'

Of course, after he said that, a new worry came to him. His mom was a smart lady. And she had a pair of sharp eyes.

Maybe she knew he had a cat.

If she did, she wasn't saying.

And he wasn't asking.

TWELVE

Clydesdale Town Hall Meeting
July 25

The town councillors held their monthly meeting. There were a lot of issues on the table. The town needed a better bus service to the big city. There were too many homeless people. And the garbage. Where was the town going to put all the garbage?

Many of the town folk attended the meeting. Even the county reporters showed up. The shop owners had a petition. 'We need to attract more people,' they argued. 'If we make High Street more attractive, it will bring in the Saturday shopping crowd.'

Those shop owners expected the mayor to pull money from a hat.

The mayor listened to the arguments. He saved the good news for last.

'The town council has received a grant to restore the High Street chapel,' he said to the crowd. 'It's an opportunity to honour our past. The fixed-up chapel can host local events, and draw tourists. We'll landscape the back garden, too.'

It was great news for Clydesdale. The street tenants and property owners wouldn't have to pay a dime. Even the reporters clapped.

'What about the lost bell?' someone called out. 'The chapel tower has been empty for generations.'

'The bell is part of this town's past,' replied the mayor. 'But we've got to have faith in the future. We'll see to the chapel first. Maybe one day, that bell will turn up.'

The town meeting was opened up to the public for a discussion. The mayor took the Chair. 'Today's public forum will be about the ferals. Clydesdale has too many street cats. Every year the problem gets worse. Four citizens have asked to speak. We'll have Mr Close up to the microphone first.'

Joe Close came to the podium. 'Most of you folk know me,' he declared to the crowd. 'The wife and I live down Haven Road by the arena. There's a pack of wild cats that hangs around the back of the bins. Those cats are nothing but vermin. One night my boy Johnny got too close to one of 'em. It scratched his hand and he had to have shots. If that ever happens again, I'm going to sue the town. I pay my taxes. My kid shouldn't have to be afraid to walk about in his own community. I say we do a cat round-up. Get rid of the ferals all at once.'

He stepped down. Some people applauded. But a girl wearing silver hoops called out, 'The ferals stay away from people. I've watched your Johnny after the squirrels. I bet he tried to hurt the cat.'

'Now now, Salome,' the mayor said. 'We'll just let everybody have their say. Keep the heckling for another occasion. Ms Winsome is up next.'

April Winsome took her time getting to the mike. She had on her best daytime dress, and a hat made of real feathers. There was powder on her nose. She said, 'There needs to be a ruling so that nobody feeds those wild cats. Why, the owner of the Lebanese restaurant leaves his bin open at nights to let them at his leftovers. Lots of other people leave out food, too. We'll have no end to the beasts unless the council takes a stand. This is a nice town. We've got to keep it that way.'

A bag lady in several dirty sweaters and a pair of flip-flops stood up. She started to mumble. The mayor jumped in quickly. 'Everyone who speaks has to have a num—'

'I'll just say my piece right here,' the lady interrupted. She spoke so quietly that the people in the room shut up and listened. 'The way I see it, *Your Honour*,' she went on, 'the town needs to take care of its own. That includes the cats. I don't want to see no cats starving on my patch.'

The reporter snapped a picture as the homeless lady hobbled out. That didn't sit well with Ms Winsome. She wanted the spotlight.

Joxie, the pet store lady, went to the stage next. 'I agree there are too many cats,' she began. 'But it's our fault. The cats are just trying to stay alive. We've got to spay and neuter the ferals. And people have to fix their pets, too. Half the time it's a wandering house cat that gets a feral pregnant. As soon as there are no more babies, the wild colonies will shrink on their own.'

She turned to the mayor. 'We should set an example for our kids. Killing off things that aren't convenient isn't the right way to go about that.'

A man in a heavy shirt almost ran over her, he was so hurried to get at the mike. His shirt must have made him hot. His red face looked ready to burst. 'Name's Gayle Lacy,' he declared. 'The way I see it, we got to do something fast and hard. There's probably more than one crazy cat lady like that Mary Downs out there. Nothing goes together better than an old lady and a bunch of street cats.

I got a birdfeeder in my back garden. If a feral stalks one of the birds, I aim to put a bat right between its pretty eyes.'

He leant right over the crowd. 'The council ought to put a bounty on their heads,' he said. 'So's I get paid for my trouble.'

The threat was applauded. 'Amen to that!' someone yelled out from the crowd.

Billy stood by the back door. He looked into the audience to see who did the yelling.

It was his dad.

THIRTEEN

Billy and his dad went back to the meadow for some more shooting.

'Takes a lot of practice to break in a gun,' his dad said. 'You bring that rag?'

Billy pulled it from his pocket.

'Let's see if we can't do more damage this time.' Billy's dad tied the rag to a sapling and got Billy to load a pellet. 'The more you practise, the more you'll get to know your trigger. All of 'em are different. Some like to take it slow. Others can't wait.'

Billy pumped up the gun. His arm was fresh, and he got to five pumps before he felt the familiar quiver of his muscles. He widened his stance and swung the barrel until the red rag lined up in the scope.

'The pellet has a long way to go before it frees

the barrel,' his dad reminded him. 'You already know the gun's going to jump when you pull the trigger. Once you learn to ride with the shot, it'll come out right.'

Billy hit the rag more times than he missed. He was sweating by the time his dad called off the practice. Only a few threads held the rag in one piece.

On the way back to the car, Billy's dad pointed to a tall oak tree. 'Take a gander up there on that branch. See the squirrel? It's time you had a live target. Want to try your luck?'

Billy looked at the red squirrel sitting in the leaves. The tail curved along the back like an armchair. It was having a meal. Bits of chaff rained down between the boughs. He shook his head. 'My arm is too tired to pump any more,' he said. 'And we're already late for dinner. Mom will be mad.'

'That woman has you scared of your own shadow,' his dad muttered. But he kept walking. As soon as they climbed in the truck he switched on the local news.

The mayor was delivering a speech. He spoke in a serious voice.

'Clydesdale citizens have asked for leadership from the council on the cat issue. The ferals are taking over our streets. These are wild animals. They keep people awake at night, and spoil the gardens. They threaten the public health. Animal Services say that it costs thirty dollars to trap a feral, and twenty more to put it down. That's too expensive for our little town. The council is asking for volunteers to help with a round-up instead. It will be held the last week of August. Cages and bait will be provided. The town will pay five bucks a head for every cat caught.'

The mayor finished up. 'Homeowners will be asked to keep their pet cats indoors for the three-day duration,' he said. 'If we round up all the cats at once, it will save the town money.'

Billy's dad punched Billy lightly in the arm. 'That mayor of ours finally found the guts to do the right thing. Those critters are pests. I'll grab a cage as soon as they come on offer.'

Billy stared out the window.

'Yes, sir,' his dad muttered. He changed the station to the baseball game. 'Be nice to get five bucks for the grey tom. That cat will buy me a beer.'

As soon as Billy and his dad got home, his folks had another row. His mom wasn't fooled when they came in the door. Maybe she could smell the gun oil. Maybe she had simply figured things out. She flung dinner on the table. Then she started up. 'He's my child too, Walter. And I say there's no need for him to learn how to shoot a gun. You know that I've never liked you hunting.'

Billy's dad wasn't having any of her arguments. He wolfed down his meal. 'I suppose you think the chicken on this plate up and volunteered to be our dinner? It's a mean world out there, Mae. Billy's got to learn that life is no picnic. And I aim to take him deer hunting as soon as I can get him a licence.'

Billy shoved his food around. His dad didn't mention the cat round-up.

'That's years away,' his mom retorted. 'Billy's too young to decide if that's what he wants.'

'He doesn't need to decide anything!' his dad yelled. 'He needs direction. Somebody's got to keep the deer population down. And it's food for the table. Just the same as this clucker.'

Billy's mom took his plate. 'Walter Reddick, your freezer's full of deer. And most of it is too old to eat.'

Billy's dad jumped up. He took a swallow of his coffee and grabbed his hat. 'You should talk,' he yelled. 'You waste time trying to "better" yourself. Meanwhile I put food on the table. You can't eat those books of yours. Till you start bringing in money again, I make the decisions in this house. I decide what the boy will do.' He stomped out.

Billy's mom cleaned up the table. She shoved a towel in Billy's hands. 'You dry the plates,' she sighed. 'Now, that's a skill you can use.' After they finished, she gathered her coat and her books.

'I'm going to the library for a bit. There's a test tomorrow. I expect you here when I get back.'

As soon as she'd gone, Billy opened his bedroom window and set Conga between his legs. Worries swirled around him. His parents acted as if they hated each other. All his friends had forgotten him. The council wanted to clean out the chapel yard. And now some people in town were gearing up to shoot cats.

'Conga,' Billy said. 'This place is going to blow like a shook-up coke can. I'll take care of you, though – no matter what.'

Conga washed her black-beaded coat. She believed him.

But Billy knew he was talking guff.

In Clydesdale, there was no safe place for a mother cat to have her kits.

FOURTEEN

August brought a heatwave.

Conga's belly was getting ripe. Her teats shone like bright pink buttons. She lost interest in games. All she wanted to do was burrow into Billy's shirt and purr like a motor on a road trip. When the grey tom stalked the back garden, she didn't pay him any attention. She was through looking out at the world. She was looking in at her kits.

One day, Billy overheard Joxie talking to her assistant in the pet store. 'A cat about to give birth is just like any other mother,' Joxie told Salome. 'One is quiet. Another screams like a banshee. That mother just has to herald the new ones.'

Right then and there, Billy made up his mind. He ran all the way back to his bedroom. 'Conga,' he huffed. 'Today's moving day. There's no use putting off what has to be. I've got an idea for a safe place. When the time comes, you can make all the noise you want.'

How could one cat need so many things? Billy rammed a foil tray into his bag along with a couple of plastic tubs. He sluiced out a juice bottle and filled it full of fresh water. On top of that he stacked kibble, cans of food and litter. There was no room left for his dressing gown, so he shoved it into a shopping bag.

Conga came out from behind the wardrobe to watch. She coiled backwards along the floor in a swollen curve. Billy reached over to rub her tummy. 'Conga,' he said. Her tail slipped round his hand and lassoed his wrist. 'Conga, you wait here. I'll come back for you once I set up your new place.' He scooped her up and put her back behind the wardrobe. Then he grabbed the bags and headed down the alley to High Street.

Salome was out the front washing windows when Billy hurried past the pet store. 'Bag boy,' she muttered.

Billy's ears went red but he kept on walking.

Behind the chapel, the ferals were having a siesta. Billy turned to look up. There was a door in the church gable high over his head. The stairs to it had long disappeared. Only the remains of a landing jutted into space. Billy set down his bags and began to stack crates along the stable wall. Once they were high enough, he climbed on to the rafters. From there he threw the belt of his dressing gown over the rail of the balcony and tied a loop. It gave him a leg up to the landing.

The door wasn't locked. He was able to walk right into the choir loft.

Billy expected to see spidery corners strewn with leftover junk. Instead, the wooden floor was swept clean. Hazy sunlight filtered through the stained-glass rosette facing High Street. The light threw patches of colour over the sloped sides of the roof and left bright stains on his clothes.

Everywhere there were cats.

Paper cats.

There must have been a hundred drawings tacked to the beams. In their charcoal skins, the paper cats walked and slept and groomed, and did a thousand different things. They sprawled in the weeds, they teetered on high wires, they leaped tall buildings and they chased their tails. In one picture, the grey tom jumped for a fence with his mouth full of vole.

'That's the apartment back garden,' Billy breathed. He wondered who else had watched the tom hunt.

Some of the drawings made Billy feel bad. There were too-thin, mangy cats with fierce eyes and snarling jaws, their mouths full of feathers and tails. There were cats with ripped ears and torn noses and smashed paws. And there were cats trapped in cages, wrapped in plastic, flattened on the road and stuffed, drowned and dripping, in trash bins.

Billy turned away. He couldn't help those cats. But he *could* help Conga.

The chapel loft was dry and warm. He pulled the things from his bag and set up a bed and a litter. He put food and water ready nearby. And he took down a few of the drawings and stacked them in the corner. Conga's newborn didn't need to see the hardship.

Before he left, Billy looked up at the empty bell tower. 'The past is a jigsaw,' his teacher had once told Billy's class during a lesson on local history. 'The bell of the old High Street chapel is a lost piece of the puzzle. Maybe it will turn up sometime.'

Billy shook his head. History wasn't important. He had Conga's future to think about.

That night, Billy told Conga all about her new home. Conga chewed his hair and hummed in his ear. When he got to talking about the bad pictures, the vibrations stopped. Her cat eyes burned like molten pennies.

'Conga, I've done my best,' Billy whispered. 'The rest is up to you.' He went to sleep right there on the floor, his top half behind the wardrobe and his feet under the bed.

There was no point in worrying about the wall-paper in the chapel.

Sometimes you had to take things as they came.

FIFTEEN

At two in the morning, Conga dug her claws into Billy's scalp. She nudged his ears. *Time*, she purred. *Time*.

Billy got up and went down the hall. His dad was snoring. He hurried back to his bedroom and got out his backpack. Conga didn't much like going inside but he stroked her ink spots until she settled in. 'It's the only way to get you out of the apartment,' he whispered. He slipped around the utility room to the kitchen door and down the stairs.

Behind the chapel, little lanterns of light floated across the yard. The ferals were out and about. Billy could see the white cat close to her little house. Soon, she'd be having kits of her own. He started his climb.

Conga growled from the mesh pocket. Billy set

his pack down gently on the balcony and swung up after it. 'Just you wait,' he soothed. 'You'll like your new home.' Softly, he pushed open the door.

He was blinded by light.

'Shut that thing!' someone hissed. 'You'll get the coppers on me.'

Billy stepped inside the choir loft and closed the door after him. For a moment he couldn't see anything but lamplight. Once his eyes settled, he picked out a dark figure hunched over a crate. It was the assistant from the pet supply store.

'I . . . I didn't know anyone was here,' Billy stammered. He searched his mind for her name. His bag squawked. A paw reached out from the pocket and hooked his shirt.

The girl jumped up. 'You have a nerve scaring me like that!' she accused. Her glittery eyes nailed him. 'And what have you got in that bag? Are you tormenting your cat?'

'No!' Billy protested. He backed into the door. The girl looked a whole lot bigger in the lamplight, her shadow filling the loft rafters over his head. And she looked ready to pounce. Salome, he remembered. Her name was Salome. He wrapped his arms around his bag. 'I'm saving her.'

The girl took a step forward. 'Let me see,' she demanded.

As soon as Billy set down the bag, Conga roared out in a huff. She stalked past Salome with her head high, acting as if she owned the place, acting as if no one else had a right to be in the church loft. Her tail lashed the air and sent shadows flickering over the pitched roof.

'Well, excuse me,' Salome drawled, getting out of the cat's way. She tossed her silver hoops and turned to Billy. 'That ball of spite looks like she stepped right out of an old Tarzan movie.'

'I've brought her here while she has her kits,' Billy explained. 'My folks don't know I've got a cat. If they find out, they'll make me take her to the shelter. Or worse.' He nodded towards the bed and litter in the corner. 'Her name's Conga. That's her stuff.'

'Conga,' Salome snorted. 'Now there's a high-priced name. You think of it all by yourself?'

Billy remembered the comic at the newsagent. 'Yes,' he lied.

The girl narrowed her eyes. 'I suppose you're the one that took down my artwork,' she challenged. 'Those drawings are my property. What was the matter? Did they hurt your eyes?'

Conga started rearranging her bed. Billy watched the cat prod the folds of his dressing gown. 'This place isn't just yours,' he said carefully. 'It's a church. Everyone has a right to be here. Even cats. This place belongs to . . . to God.'

The girl hooted. 'God moved out of here a long time ago. Now the city's in charge. And the mayor wants to give this chapel a makeover. Your cat's only got a few weeks at most to hide out before that happens.' She sat down on the crate and picked up her charcoal.

Billy watched the burnt stick scrape across a paper. 'A few weeks is all I need,' he said. 'I'll figure out something else by then.'

'Humph!' grunted the girl.

Conga let them argue. She finished inspecting her nursery and began to nose the perimeter of the loft. The dust in the corners made her sneeze. When she came to the stairway, she padded down to the main floor. Her nails clicked over the tiles of the altar platform. It was a good while before she came back up to her nest and burrowed into Billy's dressing gown.

Billy went over to her. He rubbed a pink ear. 'Conga,' he whispered. 'I've got to go. I'll be back in the morning – as soon as I can.'

Conga closed her eyes. Her kits needed the news.

'Fine friend, you are,' the girl sniffed. 'Ditching your cat in a strange place in the middle of the night.'

Billy got up and turned to face the girl. 'My folks get up early and I need to be there for breakfast,' he said. He thought for a minute, wondering whether to say what was on his mind. 'I know you. Your name is Salome. You work at the pet supply store. Maybe you can stay and watch my cat.'

Her stick of charcoal snapped in two. 'I can't help you, kiddo!' Salome scowled. 'I need to check in with the law before six in the morning, from my grandma's phone. Otherwise, I'll be a jail bird.'

Billy edged closer to look at Salome's sketch. She had drawn the chapel colony. In the picture, the cats bent their heads to the food dishes, their tails tucked close. The tom chewed blissfully, his eyes closed. Scat squatted alone in one bowl with a full mouth. Above them all, the stained-glass window of the chapel hung like a morning sun.

'The lady next door to my folks says that cats are a sign of the devil,' Billy said. 'She says that the cat is so evil, it isn't even in the Bible. You make them look like saints.'

'Not a saint or a sinner,' Salome scoffed. 'But part of God's glory.' She switched off her light. 'Let's get out of here. Your cat needs some peace.'

The two of them left as the sun came up for air. By the time the light broke free of the horizon, Billy was pulling up the covers to his bed. And Salome was climbing through a window of her grandmother's house.

In the choir loft, Conga yowled.

Her kits were done. They wanted out.

SIXTEEN

The birthing took an hour.

Conga shifted Billy's robe into a backrest. She squatted against the folds and strained. Her gut contracted. She pushed. She pushed again. Finally a steaming mess of mucus and muck plopped out. Life squirmed inside the silvery sac.

Conga knew what was needed. She cleaned her new kitten front and back. She swiped at the sticky bits with her rough tongue. The young one was nothing but a scrawny scrap of syrup shaking in the dawn air – nothing but a clammy hairball. Still, it mewled for milk as if it was made of noise. Conga nudged it close and pushed again.

Another hot handful of slop landed between the folds. Again Conga licked swiftly at the closed eyes, and a bit of pink nose. When she was done, the lump gleamed like wet coal. She strained some more.

This time she anchored her claws to Billy's gown and screeched. She arched her back. The bundle that came out was wrapped tighter than the others. It smelled sour. The little bundle twisted once before it caught the colour of dust and was quiet. Conga let it be.

One final time, she heaved. A last wobbly bit of jelly hit the mattress. Conga gave it some quick licks. As soon as it whimpered, she lay back. Her body cramped but there was nothing left worth pushing for. She was finished.

And she had three live bundles to show for all the hard work.

After a while her body settled down. She scooped her babies close and offered her teats. Moments later she felt the tugs. The soft sounds of sucking competed with her ragged pant.

At nine o'clock in the morning, Billy rushed through the loft door.

Conga regarded him contentedly. *Well*, her eyes said. *It's about time*. She lay back to let the boy admire her babies stuck to their milk straws.

'Conga,' Billy breathed. He ran out of words. The wonder of it put a cork in his throat. He hurried to set out fresh food and water. He scooped up the dead kit and took it to rest in the quiet of a hollow under the old stable. Then he went back to watch the kittens. They sprawled over each other in a heap, nuzzled close to their mother. One of them had fallen asleep with a high five in the air.

Billy let them be. It wasn't long before he fell asleep too, propped up on his elbow. The light streaming through the High Street window painted a rainbow over his face.

Conga got up and had a drink of water. Hungrily, she downed the tin of food. On the way back to her bed, she rubbed her cheek along Billy's hair.

Then she crawled in the nest and cradled her kits.

SEVENTEEN

Billy never tired of watching the kittens. One was black, one was grey and one was just like Conga. For the first few days they rolled around blindly. But one day when he walked through the loft door, the little ones looked back at Billy with their eyes wide open.

They were blue eyes.

Billy sat down and put out his hands. 'Welcome to the world,' he said.

Salome came to the chapel most nights. Most times she left behind a new sketch. One night she even wrote a note.

That grey kit will soon be roaming. Put a board across the stairs.

Billy told Luke about the kittens. The first time

Luke climbed to the loft, he stared at the drawings.

'Salome Davies drew those pictures,' said Billy. 'You know her. She works at Joxie's pet store. She's the girl who ducks behind the fish tanks whenever you walk through the door.'

Luke turned red when Billy said that.

'I could introduce you,' Billy offered.

'I've got no time for girlfriends,' Luke grunted. But he couldn't keep the admiration out of his voice when he said, 'She's got a way with a stick of charcoal.'

When Billy had to be home, and Salome was at the store, Luke offered his help. He checked Conga's water dish and changed her litter. 'Never counted on being a nursemaid,' he grumbled. But Billy knew he didn't mind the extra work.

By now Billy was a regular at Corky's. His bottle trade was making him money. All of it went on cat food and litter. Joxie shook her head. 'Between you and Luke, I'll be able to retire early.'

'Conga's eating for four,' Billy told her. He was proud of his cat. Conga never lost patience with her brood – not that her kits appreciated it. Even when she wanted to have a stretch, they hung on for dear life. They sucked and sucked as if any minute the well would run dry. Sometimes they flopped sideways trying to latch on to a teat. Or they stuck their noses into each other instead of their mom. It seemed as if they could never get enough. Conga let them wriggle and squirm and mewl. She licked off the sweet milk that soaked their bibs and filled their noses. And if they rolled away, she fetched them back.

'She's a good mom,' Billy told Joxie.

Joxie nodded. 'You're lucky then. Some mothers don't seem to bother much with their little ones. They can't tolerate the burden. They need to be out and about. Those ones want to be career cats – or night ladies.'

The chapel had mice. Every once in a while, a foolish one darted across the wooden floor. Conga became a huntress. One night as she was drowsing, the strong smell of rat filled the loft. The hairy brute slithered alongside the boards, and nibbled on the stack of paper cats. Its red eyes stared into Conga's amber ones.

Conga swelled bigger than a cushion stuck full of pins. The claws on her soft paws snuck out of their sheaths. She sucked in a growl.

The rat kept coming. It sidled forward boldly, hugging the wood, scraping the floor with its oily tail, baring its yellow teeth. It had taken on a cat before and won. A meal of new kits was worth the risk.

Conga didn't wait for it. She sprang through the air, her nails ready. The rat met her thrust with a savage lunge of his own. Fur flew. A scream tore through the dark loft.

* * *

In the morning when Billy arrived, the kits were nursing. Conga surveyed the boy placidly. The red nick on her ear glistened. As soon as he saw the blood, Billy took a careful look over the chapel, upstairs and down. He found the big rat laid open on the altar. 'Conga,' he said, after he had buried the body, 'I guess you've got some jungle left in you.'

Later, Billy told Luke about the rat. And Luke found some talk of his own.

'Snowflake is getting big,' he confided. 'Her babies are due soon. When the time comes, Joxie's going to advertise. If I'm lucky, she'll find homes for the kits. Then I'll have that cat fixed, stop her having any more.'

They were both quiet for a while before Luke spoke up again. 'I'll help you with your kits too – if and when you want. I mean.' He said the last bit in an off-hand way. 'I mean, we're mates.'

Billy nodded. He'd think on things for a bit. Soon August would be over. School would start. So far everything was working out.

Course, he didn't reckon on a smokin' gun.

EIGHTEEN

Johnny Close on Haven Street pulled the gun from the cabinet. His folks were out for the day, and he had a friend to impress. It was an air gun, decked out in army greens. The trigger was made of shiny chrome.

'I got it for Christmas,' he bragged. 'It came with cans of air. The air's already pumped up so the gun packs real muscle.'

His friend, Paul Lacy, picked it up. 'Wow! You're lucky. My folks won't buy me a gun.' He put the weapon up to his eye and pretended to shoot at a poster. 'Bam! Bam!' he shouted. 'You ever get anything with it?'

Johnny took the gun back. 'Nah. But I've been down to Lucky's Shooting Range over in Culversome. I bet I could knock out a squirrel easy.'

The two of them talked about guns for a while.

They talked about hunting. Finally Paul said, 'Your folks are out. Let's go find us some game.'

Johnny wasn't so sure about that. His mother would be hopping mad if she discovered that he'd taken the gun from the cabinet. He shook his head. 'The guy in the next house has already picked off the squirrels around here.'

His friend didn't let up. 'I never figured you for a 'fraidy cat. Maybe you don't know how to shoot. You probably never had that gun out. It's probably not even yours.' He made for the door.

'It's mine all right,' Johnny said. 'And I can shoot just fine. What have you got in mind?'

Paul turned round. 'My dad's a contractor,' he said. He sounded eager. 'The city has hired him to clean up the yard behind that dumpy little church on High Street. There's a cat colony out the back of it. His bulldozer is gonna flatten all those cats. My dad says that the city will round them up soon anyways. Let's pick off a few of the ferals right now. It'll save my dad some trouble.'

Johnny hesitated. 'People will see us.'

'Nah,' Paul snorted. 'I live over that way. There's a high fence around the place. The junk shop next door is closed on Mondays. And the folk behind the chapel are ancient. The two of them are deaf as doorknobs. Their backyard is full of trees. Nobody will know.'

Johnny couldn't make up his mind.

That riled Paul and he started to leave again. 'I don't have all day to wait while you wuss around. I guess you don't have any ammo anyway. No way your folks trust you that much.'

Bingo! Johnny got mad. His friend was right. His parents kept the pellets tucked away. But he knew where they were.

'Course I know where they are,' he bragged.

'Well, come on then,' Paul urged. 'You said that your folks were out all day. Stick the gun in your sports bag and let's get some cat.'

The more Johnny thought about it, the more it seemed like a good idea. He put a shirt around his gun and shoved it in a bag. Then he showed his friend where the pellets were hidden. 'Don't take too many,' he warned. 'My mom will notice.'

They headed out with the bag. Anybody walking down High Street would think they were just going to shoot hoops.

Billy was coming along from the other direction. When he got closer, he recognized the boys. They were in his class at school. 'Hi,' he said.

Johnny pretended to be confused. 'Hey, you know this guy?' he said to his friend.

'Nah,' Paul snorted. 'He looks a bit like our old friend, Billy. You probably don't remember him. He's too busy to hang out with his mates any more. I guess he stays home with his mommy.' He turned around and called after Billy. 'Hey, if you see Billy, tell him I left a coke bottle down by the food mart bins. He'd better hurry on over there before someone else gets it.'

Billy kept on walking. He never looked back.

'Loser!' Johnny jeered.

'Shut up,' Paul said. 'He's all right. His dad and mine are mates.'

When the boys got to the chapel yard, they thought there was some mistake. They didn't see any cats. They didn't see the ears or tails. They didn't see an eye staring through a knot hole. It looked more like a split blue glass in a grey storm

Those two wouldn't notice a cat waving a red flag.

'Someone piled up the crates by that old stable,' Paul said after a while. 'There's even a bit of rope. Let's climb up on the chapel roof and look around. We'll see better from up there.'

They clambered over the stable roof and used Billy's dressing-gown belt to get up to the little balcony. From there, they peered through the branches of the mulberry tree. Nothing in the yard moved.

Johnny was nervous. Once his folks got home, it wouldn't take them long to spot the space in the gun cabinet. 'We're wasting our time,' he said. 'There aren't any cats down there.'

Paul turned around and tried the doorknob. 'Hey,' he said. 'This door's not locked. Let's go in and look around.' He pushed open the door and squinted into the dim interior of the chapel. Something by the far wall shied away from the light.

Johnny grabbed his friend's sleeve. 'Look!' he cried. He fumbled in his sports bag and pulled out the air gun. 'There *is* a cat down there – a white one. It's by that little house thing.'

It was Snowflake. She had come out of her home in the plant pot to drink some water. Her body cramped. The kits were on their way. As soon as she heard the boys, she saw her mistake and whipped around.

She didn't stand a chance.

The shot sounded like a dull thud. Snowflake felt the pellet cut into her flank, tunnel deep through the taut string of muscle. Her leg stopped working but she kept moving. She limped back towards her pot, dragging the dead weight.

'My turn!' yelled Paul. He snatched the gun and fired. The pellet went wide.

Snowflake kept going. She made the shade. She had just a short way to go – three metres – two . . .

Johnny grabbed back the gun. 'You shoot like a girl,' he laughed.

The pellet landed squarely in Snowflake's ear just as she reached her little house.

Snowflake crawled inside. The day was growing cold.

Somewhere in the distance a siren sounded.

The wail spooked the boys. 'Gimme the bag!' Johnny cried. He dumped the gun inside. 'Let's get out of here!'

The two boys scrambled down from the balcony and raced up the chapel alley. As soon as they hit the street, they slowed right down. They acted as if they were out for a walk. When they got to the newsagent, they went in to buy a drink.

'Johnny,' bragged his friend, 'next time we take that gun, I'll blow one of those cats right out of its hide.'

Johnny shook his head. 'Aw,' he scoffed. 'You'd better stick to darts.'

Snowflake bled. All her being drained out of the hole in her ear, and the hole in her side. She could feel herself leaving. Still, she pushed. She pushed until one white kitten in a sac of light hit the straw. Snowflake couldn't see her baby but she searched with her nose. She found the warmth. She licked it clean, her tongue working even as the life left her.

Then the world went black.

There was no more time to birth the others. Snowflake and her kits had to go.

They left the white one behind to do the living.

NINETEEN

Conga flinched from the pop of the gun. As soon as the two boys disappeared, she walked through the loft door and looked over the edge of her world. A long time ago she had faced a hailstorm of gravel in a dead-end alley. The stone-thrower had promised that he would get her good.

Now he had found her. Now he was keeping his word.

She had to save her babies.

Conga grabbed a kit by the scruff of the neck. The jump to the stable roof was easy. She crawled down the crates and crossed the chapel yard. The colony cats kept to their hidey-holes while she wound between the old barrels and boards. When she reached the fence, she put all her weight on her back haunches and sprang for the rim. The kitten swung lightly from her jaws as she went up and over. She sprinted for the one place in the town where she knew that she could hide her kits – the coal cellar.

It was under the house behind the chapel.

Once upon a time that house belonged to the chapel. A preacher lived there, crammed in with his wife and six children. For a few coins and a wagon of coal, the preacher led the prayers in the chapel. The money went into the mouths of his children, and the coal went into a little room dug behind the house. A steep tin chute helped the coal fall down. On bitter winter nights, the preacher crept to his basement, opened a door and shovelled the black rock into a bucket to burn in the kitchen stove. But there was never enough. Gradually the preacher's heart grew as black and bitter as the coal. One night he packed up his family and disappeared.

So did the chapel bell.

That was a long time ago. The town grew and grew, and pretty soon the preacher's old house was just another house on Haven Street. Over the years it passed from owner to owner. They tossed trash down the coal chute – rusty engine parts, leftover garden brick, even the seat of an old Ford sedan. The last owner threw some boards over the hole and built a veranda on top.

Now Conga ran under the deck and crawled between the rotten boards. She skittered down the chute and dropped her kitten into the foam spilling from the car seat. Then she whirled around and headed back to fetch the other two. By the time she left the chapel yard with her third kit, she was getting tired. She lost her footing and bounced off the fence. Looking for an easier jump, she crossed under the mulberry tree by the old plant pot.

The smell of death waited there.

Conga stopped with her young one in her mouth. She sneered at the blood stuck to the edge of the pottery. When she crouched, she could see the still body of the white cat inside the dark interior. She could sense the tiny shape huddled close.

It was dying.

Conga jumped the fence surely. She took her third kit to the coal cellar and tucked it between the others. As soon as it was safely stowed, she headed up the chute and streaked back across the yard.

There was no time to lose.

She was a mother.

And there was one more baby out there.

TWENTY

Luke found Snowflake in a pool of blood. By the time Billy arrived, he was holding the white cat in his arms.

'Shot dead,' Luke said. 'Her little ones never saw the light of day.'

Billy looked down at the quiet cat tucked into Luke's arms. He swung his eyes up to the door in the chapel loft. It was wide open.

'Conga!' he cried. He clambered up to the stable roof. One of the old rafters split under the pounding and the raw edge clawed his leg, but he pulled himself free and up to the balcony. The loft was empty and so was the rest of the church. Billy ran back out to the landing. 'Luke, she's gone! Conga's gone. And the kits too.'

The two boys stood there staring at each other across the quiet chapel yard.

The sun shone brightly. Waves of heat shimmered in the August air. The grey tom crawled out of a crate and limbered up to the top of his castle. The other cats slipped from their nests. Scat sat up in the manger. As soon as the tom started yowling, every cat joined the chorus. They lifted their clear eyes and their wild hearts to the blue sky and the shiny sun. They cried too.

It made a woeful noise.

'I'll get a shovel,' said Luke. 'And bury this one. You go look for your cat.'

Billy ran down every alley along High Street. 'Conga,' he pleaded. 'Here girl, where are you?' He looked for a flash of white behind the bins, or a twist of bronze and black among the weeds. 'Conga!' he cried. Wherever he went, cats spilled out of shrubs and sheds. They dropped from branches and sills. But Conga wasn't there. She wasn't anywhere. Down the alley next to the Lebanese restaurant, Billy climbed through the gap in the boards on to Haven Street. He checked the gardens of the houses along the fence line, and zigzagged through the parking lot of the supermarket. He even peered under the veranda of the house behind the chapel. 'Conga,' he cried. 'Conga, are you there?'

Deep in the earth, Conga nudged her kits close. She put up her ears. She thought she heard a familiar voice on the wind. But the old coal chute turned around the sound.

And the cellar was full of the smell of coal.

By the time Billy got to the apartment, his dad was slumped over a plate of dinner. 'It's about time you got home,' his dad said. He shoved the food back and forth. 'Your mother went to the library in a huff. It doesn't take much to set her off these days. At least that fool course is over this week.' He scratched his head.

There was leftover steak-and-kidney pie on the table. The look of it made Billy feel sick.

Maybe his father felt the same way. He pushed his plate aside. 'Round-up of the ferals starts the day after tomorrow,' he went on. 'I aim to trap that grey tom. You can help me. Maybe I'll finally get a decent night's sleep.'

Billy opened his mouth. 'I'm not killing any cats!' he yelled.

Too bad he yelled the words inside his head. His father never heard a sound.

When his mom came home, his dad went out to the pub. Billy waited until his mom shut her bedroom door. Then he snuck down the back stairs and ran to the chapel yard.

Luke was waiting. 'No sign of your cat,' he said to Billy. 'I put food up there on the balcony.' He gave his friend a shrug. 'No sense in fretting. Conga's a smart one. She'll be all right. I say she's just holing out till she's sure her kits are safe. We can look again in the morning, first light. We'll find her.'

Billy swallowed hard.

On the way home, Billy saw his dad. He was outside the pub having a talk with some of his friends. Billy stuck to the shadows and crossed the street. He pressed his ear alongside the brick wall of the pub alley and listened.

'I tell you this, boys,' his dad was saying. 'Some people in the town don't like the cat round-up. Most of them live in the new homes on the north side. They don't have to listen to caterwauling night after night around the street bins and the back fences. The cats don't do business in their gardens. Now, you and I know that the fancy folk don't like the ferals any more than we do. But they want the problem to go away nicey, nicey. They don't want their conscience giving them back talk. That being the case, it's best not to speak about the round-up too much. Once the cats are gone, everyone will see the benefits.'

'Walter Reddick,' one of the men laughed, 'you oughta run for councillor. You've got a head for politics.'

'Don't know why there'll be any fuss,' complained someone else. 'Cats are only good to kick or throw down the stairs.'

Another man piped up. 'I say we shoot the things ourselves. Do it quick. The money saved can go to the homeless shelter. That should shut up the wimpy folk. And the streets will be rid of them pests. You know,' he paused, 'all this talk's given me an idea. I've a mind to do a little cat hunting tomorrow before the round-up starts. Take my boy and the Throttle. The chapel alley is a good place to start. Them devils got no right to be haunting a church back garden.'

Billy sucked in his breath. He pressed closer to the pub wall.

'Good idea,' somebody else said. 'I might do the same.'

'Best keep on the right side of the law,' Billy's dad warned. 'That said, we're not out of the woods yet. The cat lovers are putting pressure on the mayor. He might cave before the round-up begins. No telling if he'll call it off. We'll see how it goes.' He started off down the street. 'You boys have a good night.'

Billy missed the last part. He had already scooted across the street ahead of his dad. Once he was home, he sat in his room in the dark with his air rifle in his lap. As soon as his dad went to bed, he went down the back stairs again. The rifle went too.

At the chapel yard, Billy put his birthday present in the manger. He threw some leaves over it. 'Scat,' he said when the pint-sized fur ball hissed at him. 'You take care of that rifle for me.'

Billy headed out.

No one was going to shoot Conga.

Maybe his dad was right. Maybe a man needed a gun to protect what was his.

TWENTY-ONE

Billy climbed the fire escape behind the hardware store and banged on the window.

Luke came out to the landing. 'What's going on?' he demanded.

'I saw your light,' Billy said. 'Let me in.'

Luke opened the window to let Billy in. Billy didn't take notice of the room – the old glass jars and tin figures, the giant wooden barometer and the stacks of worn books. But the church plonked in the middle of the floor got his attention. The church was a miniature replica of the real High Street chapel. The tiny double doors were pinned open. A hand bell hung from the tower. And a stained-glass window decorated the gable.

The whole thing hardly came up to his waist. 'What's that?' Billy said.

'It's my project,' Luke replied.

Billy bent down to take a closer look. Some of the stained-glass pieces were pink.

'Brilliant,' Billy said. He straightened. 'But you've got to listen, Luke. There's other stuff to talk about – stuff we have to take care of right now. My dad's friends want to shoot the cats in the chapel yard tomorrow night. And the round-up is scheduled for the day after. I'm going to put a stop to all of it. Conga's still out there. You've got to help me.' He ran over to the window and peered out.

'There's nothing there,' Luke said. 'You think Conga is on my fire escape?'

'I'm looking for Salome,' Billy said. 'The hardware store under you is right beside her grandmother's garden. And the fire escape goes on up to the shop roof. I bet Salome climbs right past your window every night. Matter of fact,' he flung the door open, 'she's here right now!'

The light caught Salome red-handed on a rung of the ladder.

'About time you showed up!' Billy declared.

'For God's sake,' Salome muttered. 'Will you stop opening doors like that!' She leant against the railing and glanced past Billy. Her eyes settled on Luke.

He stared back.

'What are you two gaping at?' said Billy. 'You already know each other.'

Luke threw up his hands. 'Might as well come in,' he grumbled to Salome. 'The kid's gone crazy.'

'Hurry up,' Billy declared, shutting the door behind her. 'Snowflake is dead. Conga and her kits are gone. We've got to stop the round-up – the three of us. We have to do it tonight. I've got an idea. Listen!'

Billy Reddick must have learned a thing or two from his dad. Luke and Salome paid attention. When Billy finished talking, they both nodded. His plan made sense.

'There's a copier at the back of the hardware store,' Luke said. 'It's full of paper. And I've got a key.'

Salome patted her bag. 'I've got my pencils. I guess they'll plug those guns, all right.' She winked. 'And the windows in the City Hall dome are pure invitation.'

The light in Luke Malone's rooms stayed on all night. At four in the morning, three dark figures stole down High Street. Two of them paused at each shop window. The third one hotfooted around the back of City Hall and climbed towards the windows of the dome.

By six o'clock, the posters taped to the High Street shops had already attracted attention. A small crowd gathered around City Hall. People pointed up at the window of the mayor's office.

Some of them laughed. Others shook their fists.

A phone call got the mayor out of bed. 'You'd better get downtown,' one of the councillors insisted. 'There's a big sign plastered against the inside glass of your office. The caretaking key is gone from the hook. No one can get at it. And you've got the only other one.'

The mayor grabbed his trousers and threw on yesterday's shirt. He drove over to City Hall in a fury. Local reporters were already at the scene. A news van from the big city pulled up in front of the main doors as the mayor arrived. Someone snapped his picture.

The mayor looked up to his second-floor office. He glared at the banner plastered in his window. It was a neat bit of work. Dead cats were pinned by the neck to a line of laundry. A five-dollar price tag hung from each tail. The mayor, decked out in his official robes, was drawn at the front of the line. He had a paper bag over his head. Two kits cowered in the cage at his feet.

There were words scrawled across the top of the banner in bold letters.

Clydesdale's Shame!

The mayor fumbled in his pocket for his office key and shoved it at the morning cleaner. 'Luke! Get up there, would you, and open my office! Peel that thing off my window before we have the whole town down here taking pictures. Who got in last night anyway? Don't we lock the front doors?'

Luke shrugged. 'Night caretaker checked them all, same as usual. The only way to get inside would be through one of the windows in the dome. They don't lock any more. But who'd be up there in the middle of the night?'

Officer Jean was part of the gathering crowd. Luke's comment set off an alarm bell in her brain. She shook her head. She was being silly. Salome had checked in that morning, same as every other day. Life was full of coincidences. The girl was clearly over her roving ways.

One of the reporters shoved a mike up to the mayor's mouth. 'Does Your Honour intend to react to this protest? Or will the council let the round-up stand?'

The mayor opened his mouth before he saw the trap. No matter what he said, half of the crowd would object. He was looking at the makings of a mutiny.

So he stood there with his mouth half open.

'What'sa matter?' said the bag lady with the dirty sweaters and the flip-flops. She pushed past with a battered shopping trolley. 'Cat got yer tongue?'

TWENTY-TWO

Walter Reddick was on the roof of the house behind the chapel by six thirty that morning. The owners needed a layer of new shingle. It was an all-day job, and Billy's dad wanted an early start.

The morning breathed as gently as a baby. Reddick angled shingles over the flashing and tacked them securely. There wasn't a cloud in the sky – not unless you counted the lavender shadow suspended beyond the old chapel bell tower.

His wife had sent him to work with a packed lunch. Reddick had been surprised when Mae had slapped the tin lunchbox on the counter. She didn't make sandwiches for him much any more.

'My exam's today,' she'd said. 'It's just as well. I'm all studied out. And the maths hasn't gotten one bit easier.'

Reddick spat out a tack and hammered it into the roof. It had been a tough summer on the home front. He and Mae didn't talk together much any more, not unless one of them sparked an argument. Not so long ago, they could swap stories all night and he missed it – the talking, that is. It was his fault if you got right down to it. He'd given Mae a hard time about her schooling all summer. And Billy had gotten caught in the middle.

You had to hand it to Mae, Reddick thought grudgingly. She stuck to things. If she found a good job because of it, the extra money would benefit the whole family. He hiked up the roof a mite. 'Guess I could back off,' he muttered. 'Wouldn't hurt none.' He eyed the box of sandwiches and frowned. He hadn't thanked Mae for the work. He'd do that when he got home.

Reddick whacked another tack and mulled some more. He and Billy hadn't been getting on either. The rifle lessons hadn't helped them connect. Billy could hit a target now, no doubt about it. But whenever there was talk of hunting, the boy shut down. Reddick wiped the sweat from his forehead. The boy was a lot like his mother. Both of them were too soft for their own good. Why, guns built the country! A man without a gun was no more able to protect his family than a newborn babe.

Man needs respect, he thought. He remembered Mae's words then, words spoken during one of his rants. 'You have to respect my ideas, too.'

Maybe she was right, Reddick decided. And maybe that also went for Billy.

'What do you think of all the folderol?' he said out loud to the wandering cloud.

The shadow in the sky drifted closer. By the time it stopped moving, it was nigh over Reddick's head. Purple bruised the edges. Reddick undid a button or two and leant back against the old antenna fastened to the roof. The shade was welcomed. A few more shingles and he would climb down the ladder for Mae's sandwich.

His glance slid over to the lunchbox on the patio table.

A cat sat studying it.

Reddick squinted at the cat. It didn't look like your regular feral. It was more like a small leopard, all black and golden. 'Give it a go, you fool critter,' he jeered from his perch on the roof. 'That lunchbox's made of tin. You bring a can opener?' He raised his arm and aimed his thumb. He pretended to shoot.

The cat ignored the taunts. She just sat there studying the box. Reddick rested back against the metal tower and shut his eyes. Too bad he didn't pay attention to the cloud overhead. Too bad he didn't notice it was filling up with dark rain.

'Yowl!' The cat cried out.

Reddick opened one eye a fraction. 'What's the matter, cat? There's some reason you need my attention?' He watched her studying the box. Then he leant into the antenna and went back to dozing.

'Yowl!' The cat cried again.

'Tarnation,' Reddick complained. 'I can't even grab a catnap with all the distraction.' He opened both eyes.

The cat sniffed the sides of the lunchbox. Slowly, she began to circle, nosing one side of tin. She looked up to make sure the man on the roof was watching. Then one bronze paw gave the box a poke.

Reddick tensed. 'I'd be out hunting for a new town if I were you,' he yelled, 'instead of trying to nab my lunch! This time tomorrow you'll be behind bars.'

His threat fell on deaf ears. The cat had focused on her prey. She nudged the box against a crooked slat in the table. As soon as it caught, she shoved the latch sideways with her paw. Presto! The lunchbox swung open.

'Blast it!' Reddick swore. He scrambled to his knees away from the antennae – away from the metal rails. He *let go*.

So did the cloud. It had stretched as much as it

could. Now it cracked apart.

Maybe it was the heat bouncing off the peak of the roof. Or maybe Reddick's rage ignited the cloud. Whatever the reason, a thread of lightning cut a crooked path through the hot air and zeroed in on the antenna. It struck with enough voltage to snap the metal in two. White-hot flames blazed up.

Reddick threw himself away from the heat. Rolling to the edge of the steep roof, he jumped for his life. He was no cat. He could have snapped his neck. Only the junipers planted around the deck set him down easy.

The whole show was over in a matter of seconds. The wounded cloud bled buckets of rain. The roof got wet, Reddick got wet, and so did the cat. As soon as the cloud drained dry, it trailed away like a rag shot to smithereens.

The water had made short work of the flames. Reddick was still staring at the smouldering hole in the house's roof when the cat jumped right over his head. She tore out of the juniper bushes with his sandwich in her mouth.

The sorry truth hit Reddick like a round of buckshot.

All that yowling was done for a purpose. That cat had seen the future. That cat had saved his life.

'Dammit cat!' Reddick scrambled to his feet and shook his fist. He yelled to the empty yard.

'Dammit cat, you can keep the sandwich!'

There was no way Reddick was climbing back on the roof again that day. He grabbed his ladder and jammed it under the veranda. Then he drove to the hardware store to phone the fire department. 'I'll need more than shingles to finish the roof now,' he told the hardware store owner after he had finished telling his story.

The owner had a story of his own. 'Did you see the news, Walt?' he asked.

Reddick was still thinking about the cat. 'What news?' he muttered.

'Here.' The owner shoved the local newspaper into his hand.

Reddick almost laughed out loud. The picture on the front page showed a bunch of placard-waving people around the steps of City Hall. All the signs said the same thing.

Save the cats. Stop the round-up!

'It's no laughing matter.' The hardware man sounded upset. 'The people in that picture don't look like folks around here. I'll wager most of them have come from the city to make trouble. Those people have no business interfering in the affairs of our town.'

The hardware man had a point. But he had paid no mind to the facts. Reddick recognized some of

the faces. Those people worked in the neighbour-
hood. But the hardware shop owner expected
Walter Reddick to agree with him anyway.

Reddick took a closer look at the paper. The kid
with his back to the camera looked familiar. In
fact, it looked a lot like his Billy. For once, he kept
his mouth shut.

He paid for his nails and got out.

Conga ate the sandwich ravenously. Then she
scurried back to her nest in the coal cellar. Her
young 'uns needed a meal too. Only something
was wrong. Something blocked her way. Metal
bars crossed the hole in the boards. She couldn't
get into the chute. She couldn't get to her kits.
'Myuuuuur!' she cried.

The kits mew-mewed back. They wanted their
mother. They wanted milk.

Conga railed at the ladder rungs in her way. She
stuck her paw through a crack and clawed the
dark air. Back and forth under the veranda, she
searched for another way into the cellar. It was no
use. Finally she stuck her nose between the bars
and commanded her kits.

'Myuuuuur!'

It took a while for the kits to decode the
message. Their mother's cry sounded far away.
One by one they toppled over the side of the old
car seat. The slippery slope of the chute was

another challenge. The grey led the charge. Near the top, he lost his footing and bowled his sisters over. All the kittens ended up in a quivery heap at the bottom. They had to start their climb all over again.

The white kit was too little to make the journey. It huddled between the springs of the Ford seat. All it knew was how to wait.

Conga coaxed her kits. When each one stuck their heads between a rung and a board, she pinched their skin between her teeth and hauled them out. Briefly she let them nurse. Then she began to dig. Her back paws flung dry clods of earth and stone chips against the veranda over her head. Back and forth, her paws scraped at the hard ground.

Several inches down, she came to the outside wall of the coal chute.

It was made of tin.

TWENTY-THREE

Conga dug. Luke scraped the poster off the window in the mayor's office. Salome kept her grandmother company at the breakfast table. Billy looked for his cat.

It was seven in the morning and the new day was well on its way.

Billy walked along High Street. The doorways and windows of the shops were plastered with Salome's work. Only a few of the drawings had been ripped away. The posters showed the mayor with five-dollar bills stuffed in his collar, and falling from his pockets. On the one at Corky's, someone had added a moustache to his stiff upper lip. The ends of the moustache stuck out like cat whiskers.

Billy avoided the cameras at City Hall. He gave Luke a small backhanded wave as he pushed past the mob milling outside the front doors. The mayor looked madder than a March hare. Good, thought Billy. Maybe the council would get the message. Maybe they would see that the cats needed help.

As for his dad's mates and their plans – well, Billy had a gun, too.

He needed to find Conga. He tried to think like his cat. He tried to *be* her. Where would she go? He knew where she liked to hide – in his dressing gown, in his boots. There was nothing like that in people's back gardens. Billy scoured the alleys one more time without luck. Conga had disappeared from the face of the earth.

How could he know she was digging a tunnel to the middle of the world?

By eleven in the morning, Billy couldn't fight his need for sleep any longer. He went home. He expected ructions when he opened the door. He expected his mom to be waiting in the kitchen with her arms crossed, biting her bottom lip. Or maybe his dad would be there instead, one hand clenched around a cup of cold coffee. So it was a surprise to find the apartment empty, and his bedroom door as he always left it – shut.

Billy crawled under the covers where it was dark. He slept. Around dinnertime, the sound of low chatter roused him, and he hurried out of bed. There was packing to do. He found his dented old flashlight and clipped it to his belt. He emptied his money jar. This time he wasn't coming home again – not without his cat – and not as long as the whole town was up in arms.

His folks were in the kitchen. When Billy eased open his bedroom door, the smell of fish and chips made his stomach growl. Billy sucked in the rumblings. Conga was probably hungry, too. He stood in the hall behind the utility room waiting for a chance to get past his parents and escape out the kitchen door.

'I don't know why they can't set an exam that makes sense,' his mom was complaining. 'I failed the maths paper for sure.'

Billy waited for his dad to put his mom down. He waited for his dad to say, 'I told you so.' He waited for one of them to stomp out. It made Billy tired all over again – the waiting for it.

Only his dad didn't say, 'I told you so.' Instead he said, 'Mae, the way I see it, life is too short to cry over spilt milk. You can take the maths again if there's a need.'

Billy barged into the middle of the kitchen in a big hurry. He thought his dad was sick. Maybe his dad was so sick he was going to die. 'Well, it's about time you got up,' his mom said to him. 'You spend too much time in that room of yours. Have some dinner. You can keep me company tonight when your dad goes to the pub.'

Billy looked his dad over from top to bottom. He looked the same as always. 'Maybe tomorrow,' Billy said and streaked out the door.

'What's got into him?' his mom said. 'The boy looks like he just lost his best friend.'

His dad shook his head. He had something to get off his chest. 'Mae, I've got to tell you,' he said. 'A cat saved my life today – a real smart cat with a taste for homemade sandwiches.'

Billy's mom sat down at the table. 'How's that?' she said.

That's when Billy's dad told Billy's mom the whole story. He told her about the jungle cat that could open lunchboxes, and he told her about roof-jumping away from the bright white flames. When the story was over, he reached for her hand. 'I guess that was the best sandwich you ever made me, Mae,' he told her. 'I owe you. I owe the cat, too. It's a bad business to be beholden to one of them critters.' He moved his hand to touch her hair. 'There's something I've got to tend to right now. But I'm hoping you'll wait up for me.'

Billy's mom sat very still. Finally she put her hand on her husband's forehead. 'You feeling feverish, Walt?' she asked.

Luke had fed and watered the ferals by the time Billy got to the alley. Salome stood on the little balcony. 'The two of you go and look for Conga,' she called down when Billy rounded the chapel corner. 'I'll wait in the loft with a can of food in case your cat decides to drop by.'

Billy and Luke headed out with the flashlights. They split up and got on with the job of finding a mother cat in a town full of strays.

Maybe they believed that needles stuck out of haystacks.

Once they were gone, Salome went into the choir loft. She slumped against the slope of the roof, pulled Billy's dressing gown over her shoulders and opened a tin of cat food. The air darkened around her.

It had been a long day. After breakfast Salome had gone to the pet store as usual. Joxie was full of talk. 'Funny how that big sign found its way into the mayor's office in the dead of night,' she had said. 'The only way to get in would be through one of the windows in the dome.' Joxie had peered suspiciously at Salome. 'Girl, you've got dark circles under your eyes. It looks to me like you're missing sleep.'

Sitting in the choir loft, Salome reached into her bag for her notepad. Before she had her pencil drawn, her eyes got heavy. By the time Billy came back to the chapel yard, she was dreaming in charcoal. She didn't hear Billy fishing in the manger. And when he got to the loft with his burden, she didn't have questions.

Billy stuck a pellet in the chamber. He clicked the rifle in place and sat down next to a crack in the loft door. It was nine o'clock. He hadn't found Conga. The mayor hadn't called off the round-up. And it was almost dark.

Time was up.

Under the veranda, Conga scrabbled dirt away from the outer side of the tin chute. Her work wasn't worth much. The clay along the chute was well packed, and she had to dig around chunks of rock. The old wound in her paw tore wider with the wear. Blood mixed with the stones and dirt.

All the while the kits harassed their mother. They tugged at her haunches, and crawled under her belly. She stopped long enough to fill them with milk. She took more precious time to find water in a bit of drainpipe. Before she went back to her digging, she called again to the little white kitten.

There was no answer from the cellar. Nothing stirred in the foam nest of the Ford seat.

The waiting was near over.

Time was up.

The boys at the bar already had their drinks in hand by the time Reddick arrived.

'I'll wait till midnight,' Joe Close was saying. 'I'm bringing Johnny along. He can watch his pa bust those pests. I might even let the boy take a shot of his own. I bought him an air gun, a real little beauty, for Christmas. Took him down to Lucky's Range a few times. The boy's set to go.'

The man with the red face ordered a second beer. 'There's a rumour that the mayor's getting cold feet,' he griped. 'My bet is he'll pull the round-up afore it starts. Maybe I'll give you and your boy a hand at the chapel. Show you a trick or two. There's more than one way to skin a cat.'

The men all shifted to let Billy's dad fit at the table. 'Hey, Walt,' said the man with the red face. 'I heard you had a bad moment on the old chapel house roof today. Glad to see you're all right. A bit of cat-hunting might lighten your mind.'

Reddick chugged back his brew. 'Gayle, I've already put the day behind me. As for your hunting plans tonight, that's asking for trouble. The press is nosing around. We don't want the town to get a bad name.'

The men guffawed. 'Walter, that's the first time I ever heard you care what anyone thought,' one of them joked. 'Next thing you know, you'll be siding with the ferals.'

Reddick didn't answer. The beer tasted like sawdust. Curse that cat. He took a long dry swallow and shoved his chair back. 'I've changed my mind,' he said. 'The way I see it, the cats—'

He didn't get any further. The bartender

pointed to the screen over the bar. 'Looks like the cats get a reprieve,' he declared. 'Round-up's cancelled.'

Joe Close slammed his fist on the table. 'The mayor's a wimp,' he declared. 'And my mind's made up.' He looked Reddick in the eye. 'The old chapel's crawling with ferals. My boy and I are hunting cat tonight. I don't want to hear any more lax talk.' He walked out.

Reddick watched him. He let the conversation swirl around him as he reviewed his day. The house he was working on backed on to the chapel yard. Maybe that fool cat sheltered there. The more Walt thought about that the more he faced what he had to do. He stood up and slapped a twenty-dollar bill on the table. 'I think I'll have an early night,' he said. 'You boys have another round on me.'

As soon as the pub door slammed shut, Reddick turned towards the chapel alley. He'd take a shot at finding the cat ahead of Joe and his boy.

He had a debt to pay.

Time was up.

TWENTY-FOUR

Down in the yard, the cats took their night stations. The three copycats climbed into the low branches of the mulberry tree. Mac and Cheese hunkered down between the rafters of the stable roof next to Nosy Parker. And Scat shredded the manger scraps into a cloud woolly enough to fill the space left by a gun already taken.

On top of his castle of crates, the grey tom scanned the alley. The moon turned his coat into silver armour. When the boy and the man showed up, he eased into the shadows.

'There!' said the boy. He pointed to the crates. 'There's a cat up there. It's a big one. Got eyes like slick ice. Get it, Dad!'

'Easy as pie,' Joe Close nodded. 'You get over towards the old stable, away from the mulberry tree. I'll back up a bit the other way. We'll coax that brute into the open.' He handed his son the gun, and reached into his pocket for the shot. 'Load her up. Keep the cat in your sight.'

'Now, hold on, Joe.' The quiet warning sliced through the dark yard. Walter Reddick stepped into the moonlight. He stood with his back to the alley, his hands up.

Johnny's father spun round. 'Walt!' he declared. 'You gave me a start. What are you doing here? My boy and I will take care of these cats. You go on over to City Hall, if you want to see fur fly.'

'No call for a gun in a chapel yard,' Reddick said. He took a few steps deeper into the yard. 'Why don't you two—'

'There it is!' Johnny interrupted. 'C'mon, Dad. Hurry! It'll get away.'

The grey tom darted from the shadows and sprang up to a fence post. He waited there, his eyes glittering, his shoulders hunched, waited until the three pairs of eyes held his own. Then he began to slink along the lip of the fence away from the yard. He moved deliberately, stopping every few steps to look back.

It was an outright dare.

'Shake a leg, boy!' Joe Close hissed. 'Duck around the tree. That cat thinks we're stupid. Once you get a clear view, line it up in your scope. I'll grant you one shot. Takes more than that to rouse people from their beds. Don't waste it.'

Johnny cut through the stable. He hurried out past the old manger and readied his gun.

Reddick reached down and swiped a stone from the chapel earth. He drew back his arm.

'Get away from the cats!' The words fell from the sky.

Reddick's arm froze in mid motion. There was someone outlined against the moon over his head. Someone had come out of the choir loft. It looked like a boy. It looked like his . . . 'Billy!' Reddick called out. He dropped the stone. 'Billy, put down that gun!'

Billy was so focused that he didn't even hear his dad. He swung up his rifle easily. He'd had a lot of practice.

Joe Close couldn't see the boy. But he heard the rifle cock. He yanked Johnny under the stable cover. The commotion riled the cats hiding in the rafters. They jumped every which way.

It was cat rain.

Joe Close threw up his arms when one furry beast brushed his face. The reflex spun Johnny into the manger. That sent Scat off like a cannon. The scraggy bolt of rage shot from his woolly bed and latched on to the back of Johnny's head. As soon as the boy felt claws digging into his scalp, he started to dance. He stomped his feet so fast he forgot about his fingers.

The gun in his hand didn't need more coaxing.

It went off.

In the same instant, Salome bolted out to the loft landing. 'Fool!' she yelled. She grabbed Billy by the collar.

Billy fired too.

Both bullets found a mark.

Johnny shot himself in the foot.

And Billy shot his dad.

TWENTY-FIVE

The pellet grazed Billy's dad's arm.

Reddick looked down at himself in surprise. He watched the dry burn darken. A drop of blood welled up.

'Dad,' Billy cried. He threw the rifle down to the yard and hurtled after it. He didn't stop his headlong dash until he had run right into his dad's arms. 'Dad, are you okay? I'm sorry. I'm sorry!' His sobs were full of grief, full of anger.

'Hold it right there, son,' his dad said. He gripped Billy at arms' length so they could look at each other. 'I'm all right, you hear me? Simmer down! I'm to blame for what's happened here.'

Johnny Close hopped over the yard yelping louder than a cat on a hot tin roof. 'That's enough!' Reddick called out. 'You're all right, boy. Take off that shoe. Your boot has a steel toe.

You've got nothing more than a hot foot.' He turned to Joe Close. 'Your kid needs to go home,' he growled. 'And mine. We're done here.'

As soon as the other two had left, Billy blurted it out. 'They wanted to kill my cat.' He didn't care if his dad knew the truth.

Billy's dad tilted his boy's chin. He didn't want to believe in Providence. But he was too sensible to ignore bare facts. 'What did you say, son? What do you mean, your cat? You've got no cat.'

'I do!' Billy cried. 'I've got Conga. She's my cat. I had her in my room the whole summer. And now she's out there with her kits and it's my fault. I have to find her!' He pushed his dad's arms away. 'Conga!' he yelled. 'Where are you? Conga!'

The wild shriek shut him up. A she-cat materialized on the top of the fence. She ran at the grey tom, backing him into the post by the edge of the yard. Then she gave Billy one of her looks.

'Conga!' Billy yelled. 'Conga, wait!' He could have saved his breath. The cat vanished over the far side of the fence. Billy ran across the yard, kicking at the crates, scrambling up the sides. 'That's her!' he cried. 'That's Conga. She wants me to follow her. I've got to get over the fence! Dad, help me!'

Billy's dad didn't hesitate. He picked up his boy and dumped him over the boards.

'Wait for me!' a girl shouted. Reddick practically

jumped out of his skin. He looked up to a mulberry branch spreading over his head. A black ghost hustled along the limb. She was nothing more than a hurried shadow blocking the star-spangled sky but it didn't take a genius to know she was headed after his Billy. He reached for the rim of the fence.

'Stop right there!' another voice shouted.

Criminy! Reddick cursed. There was someone else in the yard. He spun into the glare of alien eyes. They were headlights, fierce yellow ones. A bulldozer had rumbled into the alley. The dull drone of the motor swelled into a vibrating roar as it squeezed between the narrow walls.

'Stop!' the voice yelled again. In front of the headlights, a figure waved his arms wildly.

'Oh God, Luke!' the girl in the tree shouted, hooked to a swaying limb by her knees. 'That thing is bigger than you! Get out of the way.'

'It'll have to flatten me first!' the figure bawled back.

Billy's dad recognized the dark shape in front of the lights. It was the ponytailed kid, the street boy, the one always picking in the bins. He was trying to stop a bulldozer from coming into the chapel yard. Idiot! Did he think he could stop ten tons of steel?

The dozer rolled relentlessly down the alley, closer and closer. The man with the red face leaned out the window. 'Get out o' there,' he yelled at the boy blocking his path. 'The council wants this place cleaned up. I've got a contract. You can't obstruct the city.'

'Over my dead body!' Luke yelled. He stood his ground.

'Oh, brother!' muttered Salome, dropping from her perch over Reddick's head. 'This is really gonna land me in the clink.' She sprinted towards the boy and linked her arm through his. 'Make that two bodies!' she yelled at the bulldozer. She stamped her foot at the hungry shovel. Her silver hoops flashed.

The driver leant out of the window. 'No kiddies gonna stop me from doing my job!' he bellowed.

'In the name of reason!' Reddick grunted. He left the fence, clambering over the crates and barrels, the pottery house, shoving his bulk between the girl and the ponytailed kid. 'Cut that motor!' he ordered the driver. 'Before someone gets hurt.'

'*Yowl!*' The scream rode over the roar of the machine. Reddick felt the hair on his neck stand up when a heap of wire bristles shoved between his feet. The grey tom had joined the party. The cat took up a stance at the front of the line.

The bulldozer kept coming.

'*Yowl!*' the tom screamed again. His blue eyes chilled the fierce machinery.

Two metres from the blockade, the man in the bulldozer gave up. He cut the engine and climbed out of his cab. 'Hey, Walt!' he said. 'What brings you out in the middle of the night? You turn into some bloody tree-hugger?'

Billy's dad looked down. The grey tom was gone. So were the kids. He was alone. 'I guess I keep company with ghosts,' he said to the man planted beside his bulldozer. 'It's turning out to be a long night. And I want to go home. I suggest you do the same. You and I can have it out tomorrow. I'll buy the beer.' He folded his arms and waited.

The driver put his hands on his hips and did some waiting of his own. The chapel yard got real quiet. It could have been the stage set of an old western, it became so still.

The two men sized each other up. Anybody would think they were gearing for a showdown, the way each tried to outstare the other. All they needed were a pair of hats and a couple of packed holsters. Good thing they decided to use their heads instead.

The driver stood down first. 'Well, Walt,' he said. 'A man can yield a little for a free beer.'

'Call it a night right now,' said Billy's dad, 'and I'll make it two.'

They left the bulldozer in the alley.

TWENTY-SIX

Billy was aiming to catch a cat on the run.

He wound through the trees until he was close to the old chapel house. The air smelt faintly of burnt matches. Somewhere beneath the deck, he could hear the gritty splash of sand hitting wood. Billy stuck his flashlight under the boards. There wasn't much to see – a wheelbarrow, some lawn furniture, a ladder . . .

Six tiny mirrors reflected the torchlight. He had found the kits.

Billy rolled under the veranda and squirmed over to the pile of warm kittens. He scooped them close. A spray of stone chips stung his cheek, and he aimed the light into the source. Something was digging. 'Conga!' he called out. 'Conga, is that you?'

Her tail was sticking out of a hole. When he

reached over to haul her out, she swiped a paw across his hand. Billy stared at the trail of blood. It wasn't his blood. It was hers. What did she want? Why was she digging? 'Conga,' Billy coaxed. 'You can stop that now. Your kits are here. We're going home.'

Conga didn't let up. Her front haunches worked like tired pistons, scratching at the rocky earth alongside the coal chute. Billy couldn't figure it out. His cat wanted to go right through a tin wall. Maybe there was something in the old coal cellar. Maybe it was a mouse or a rat. He scanned his light over the opening. Ladder rungs blocked the entrance.

Billy was his daddy's boy. He didn't waste time with questions. 'Okay, Conga,' he said. 'I don't know what's down there. But I'll help you get to it.' He wrenched the ladder loose.

Conga darted past him. She headed into the blackest night.

Now what?

Billy waited. He tried to be patient. The kits mewled and he chucked them into his lap, kneading their soft bodies until they melted into a sleepy puddle. He waited some more. 'Come on, girl,' he pleaded. 'Conga, come on.' He stuck his eye to the hole. 'Hurry up and come back,' he cajoled. He pursed his lips and tried to sweet-talk his cat up the chute.

Kiss, kiss, kiss.

None of it was any use.

Billy waited until he was done waiting. He settled the kits down on the floor and attacked the rest of the cover. The splinters of the old boards jabbed his skin. The shards ripped his hands. When the last piece of wood gave up, he stuck his head and shoulders into the hole. The darkness gobbled the light of his flash

Billy didn't want to go into a deep dark hole. But he meant to find his cat. He started down.

The shaft was just big enough for him to wriggle along on his belly. He stuck his elbows into the corrugations for grip. 'Conga,' he whispered. 'Where are you?' His voice sounded faint in his ears, as if the sound was coming from far away. Near the bottom of the shaft, he dropped into a little room. On his knees, he tried to make sense of the space. The vault was crammed with junk – old shovels, picks, a garden chair. There was a car bumper and part of an old sink. There was a bucket and some coal. But where was Conga? He panned his light.

She lay on her side in some bits of foam. Billy crawled closer. A white kit was buried in her belly, getting milk, sucking hard.

'Conga,' Billy breathed. 'Where did *that* kit come from?'

Conga looked at him. Her eyes dripped honey.

That was the last thing Billy saw before his flashlight went out. The cellar turned black as a tomb. Billy didn't care. 'Wicked!" he whispered. 'Conga, we're going out now. I don't need any light. I know the way.' He flung the cylinder into the blackness,

The heavy flashlight rocketed across the cellar true as an arrow. It slammed right into a bell, an old chapel bell.

Bong! The loud chime reverberated against the tin walls. It rattled the shovels and picks, the springs of the Ford seat, the old bumper. The peals rang up the chute and poured music into the fresh night.

Salome stood on the veranda listening to the well-spring beneath her feet. 'Oh. My. God!' she exclaimed.

'What?' said Luke. He bent down to look under the side of the deck. 'What's that ringing?'

Salome crossed her arms. Men, she thought. They can't see what's right in front of their faces. 'That, Luke,' she said, 'is the sound of your miracle.'

'Hey!' Billy called up to them. He wriggled out from under the deck. After the dark of the tunnel, the stars in the sky twinkled as bright as budding suns. 'Hey!' he said again. 'Look, you guys! I've got Conga. Her kits are here, too.' He opened his hands to show them the white one. 'And she's got another baby!'

'Well,' said Salome. She looked as smug as a cat with the cream. 'I guess there are miracles all round.'

Billy didn't wait to find out what she meant. He fetched the kits and headed home.

Conga rode rifle on his shoulder.

TWENTY-SEVEN

The mayor held an emergency session with the Clydesdale councillors. He was in high dudgeon. The town was so divided over the cat issue, the whole mess threatened to ruin his chances in the next election. 'We've got to get a handle on this thing,' said the mayor. 'First I had to cancel the round-up. Now I've got to put the clean-up of the chapel yard on hold. Everybody in this town has something to say. Why look at 'em!' He pointed to the table. It was covered in letters, emails and messages. 'Every one wants something different.'

The mayor snatched a paper. 'Listen to this one,' he said.

Email: jboy@hotmail.com
See here, Mr Mayor. I don't want my hard-earned

money going into some cat shelter. I've got kids that need shoes. This town needs jobs. It needs more people to visit and spend their money. The cats give the town a bad name. Shoot them, trap them, drown them, starve them – whatever gets rid of them!

I'd sooner let a mosquito suck my blood than help a feral. You boys up there at City Hall have lost my vote. Our town needs decent direction.

The mayor tossed the email back on the pile. He waved another letter. 'This one's the flip side of the coin,' he declared.

Dear Mayor,

Bounty indeed! Are we going to kill the robins and the sparrows for defacing our streets? Shoot the gulls that come in from the sea when the weather changes? How about the squirrels – and those dirty rabbits?

I'll say one thing. Come election time, you've lost my vote. And if anyone comes on my property looking to nab a cat, I'll post their picture on my blog – right along with yours. I get a thousand hits a day on that blog.

We need decent leadership. Our town has lost its way.

Yours truly,
Lucie Morton

'See what I mean!' the mayor blustered. 'I tell you we have to come up with—'

The mayor's assistant came into the council chamber. 'There's a delegation to see you,' she said to the mayor.

'Not now!' the mayor replied, waving his hand. He waved his hand so hard it looked like he wanted to sweep his assistant under the table. 'There's no time to see anyone. The council has to solve this cat thing before every newspaper in the country sets up shop in Clydesdale. The ferals have got us between a rock and a hard place.'

'You mean between a coal cellar and a lump of coal,' a voice drawled.

The mayor swung round. So did the councillors. Salome Davies, Mrs Davies's granddaughter, was leaning against the council-room door. She had on a funny get-up as usual – tight black clothes and shiny hoops in her ears. The pony-tailed young man from maintenance was there too, and another kid. The mayor searched his memory. It was Walter Reddick's son, Billy.

The mayor did some more handwaving. 'You three can't interrupt my meeting,' he said. 'Billy, if you have a school project, my assistant can let you have whatever information you need. Luke, don't you have work to do on those loose windows up in the dome? And Salome, as far as I know, your grandmother doesn't like you straying too far from home.'

'Mr Mayor,' said Billy, 'it's August. School hasn't started yet. We've come to talk to you. We've got a proposition for the council.'

'I wrote to you about it,' Luke added. 'You might want to consider the idea now.'

The mayor could feel his temper in his eyeballs. He didn't have time to listen to some childish scheme – not while his picture was plastered on every High Street shop; not when he might end up the laughing stock of the whole county. 'Enough!' he exploded. 'Now you all get out of here and let us—'

'I guess the old chapel bell can hide out for ever,' Salome drawled to Billy and Luke. 'Come on. The mayor isn't interested in our discovery. Let's get out of here.'

They turned away.

The mayor was no fool. At the sound of the word 'bell', his mouth began to water. He was out of his chair before the three of them reached the stairs. 'Wait!' He plastered a smile across his face. 'Why don't we all go into my office for a chat?' he wheedled. 'My door is always open. I'm always ready to hear from my constituents.'

His hand swept them up. He was a good sweeper. As soon as they were seated in his office, he leant forward across his desk. 'A bell, you say?'

'First things first,' Salome said. She unrolled a paper.

The mayor studied it. 'That drawing reminds me of the town,' he said slowly.

'It's a model – a pint-sized version of High Street,' said Luke. 'I want to build it behind the chapel. The cats can shelter there.'

'A cat home!' the mayor snorted. 'We can't even afford to get people off the streets. Who's going to look after something like that?'

'I will,' said Luke. 'I've already got a couple of volunteers.' He set down his package and pulled away the wrapping. The little bell tower was inside. The tiny hand bell swung from the belfry. 'This is some of my work.'

'It's a good idea to rally the town,' Salome said to the mayor before he could protest. 'All the city has to do is encourage people to mind their pets. They need education. Lots of places have a cat problem. Our town can be an example. Other city councils will be running to see how you do it.'

'Half the town hates the cats,' the mayor argued. His voice strangled in his own throat. He liked the tower. The kids had a point.

Salome didn't let up. 'The council already has the money to restore the chapel,' she said. 'Luke's cat sanctuary will attract tourists, too. They'll spend money in the shops and eat in the restaurants. Some of them might even decide to settle.

My grandmother says what's good for the cats is good for all.'

The mayor hemmed and hawed. 'Maybe she's right,' he said finally. 'That grandmother of yours always was a straight shooter. Now, what's this about a bell?'

Salome looked at Billy. Luke looked at Billy, too. It was Billy's turn to speak.

'We need an agreement before I tell you where the bell is,' Billy said. 'You need to talk to the council.'

Salome grinned. 'My grandmother's bringing her lawyer,' she told the mayor, 'soon as you decide. So nobody pulls a fast one.'

Billy's mom and dad were at the kitchen table when he got home. They were talking in a comfortable way.

'Glad you could join us,' said his mom. 'I made some of that potato salad you're always on about. Your father helped me peel the potatoes.'

Conga and her kits were taking in the late sun that slanted through the porch window. Conga's eyes were half closed. Her front paws were swaddled in strips of cloth. The white kit slept between the bandages.

'Billy,' his dad said slowly. 'I know we have some mending to do. Maybe I should have asked you how you felt about the gun. I wanted to teach you the same way as my dad taught me.' He gestured toward the air rifle propped up beside the closet.

Billy looked towards the rifle. But his gaze slid right by it. He fetched his dad's toolbox to the table. 'Dad,' he said, 'I'm going to help someone with a project. It'll take a while. Maybe you can teach me how to use this.' He handed his dad the hammer.

It was a beautiful tool. The warm hickory handle ended in a steel cap and claw.

'Well,' his dad said, sitting up a little taller. He smacked the hammer lightly against the palm of his left hand. 'You've come to the right man. A hammer is all about control. The nail has to go in straight. If your aim is off, you might as well be splitting logs. You've got to know what you're hitting too. Too much force will . . .'

'Men,' muttered Billy's mom. She handed Billy the potato salad. 'I'll never understand them.'

They were smiling words.

TWENTY-EIGHT

It was the second Sunday before Christmas.

People began to gather in the light snow. At three o'clock the mayor arrived on foot. He went up to the double doors and knocked. As soon as the doors swung open, everyone flocked inside the chapel. Straw matting was strewn over the newly varnished floor. There were cups of cheer over the table. Mae Reddick held up a plate of cookies.

Salome leaned over the chapel railing and watched the townsfolk admire the renovations. Gradually people climbed the stairs to join her in the choir loft. The winter light streaming through the stained-glass window coloured the art nailed to the walls. The charcoal drawings were framed in bright red. A price tag hung from each corner.

'Those cats look real enough to give me

allergies,' someone declared. 'I hear the proceeds from this sale will be donated to cat rescue.'

'The artist is a real credit to her grandmother,' a friend agreed.

'Congratulations!' said Officer Jean to Salome. 'I'll buy this one.'

Salome nodded. It was her favourite. A cat curled around blank space. There was no way to tell if it was alive or dead, sated or hungry, warm or cold. It slept mindlessly between heaven and earth.

'Your drawings might be worth a fine penny some day,' Officer Jean went on, as Salome wrapped up the little picture. 'But I don't care about that. This is a darned good piece. I'm glad you decided to put your talent to work instead of climbing about in other people's places.'

'Yes,' agreed Mrs Davies. She gave her grand-daughter a hug. 'Salome was good company last summer. She never caused me a moment's worry. Even her folks say she's a changed girl. The whole family's coming to stay for Christmas.'

'Humph!' Joxie sniffed quietly. She took the picture of a pregnant cat off the wall. 'This one will go in my shop. Maybe it will remind customers of the true meaning of the season.'

Two of the councillors wandered through the choir loft. One of them said, 'These drawings look familiar. I feel as if I've seen them before.'

'Beats me,' said the other. 'I don't know much about art. The girl is good. That's about all I can tell you.'

The mayor called out. 'It's time to dedicate Clydesdale's newest project.' He led the people out of the double doors and down the alley. His hand swept across the chapel yard.

'Somebody shrunk the town,' the man with the red face snorted.

It was true. A tiny copy of High Street stretched along the back fence. Joxie's pet store was there. And so was the apartment building. Even Corky's and the Lebanese restaurant had a place.

There was a sign affixed to the mulberry tree.

'Cat Haven'

'Nice job, Walt,' said Joe Close. 'That little apartment looks so real, I expect Mae to peek out of a window.'

'Billy and I followed directions,' Billy's father said. 'The town planner is over there.' He pointed at Luke. 'That young man is going places. All he needs is a haircut.'

Luke stood behind the picket fence fixing the latch to the gate. A lady in a fancy fur hat reached over to shake his hand.

The cats were outside their shelters, eyes drowsy, tails slack, smudging their coats with their raspy tongues. A name hung over each door. Scat's manger filled up the City Hall. Pickerel, Perch and Pike had the apartment rooms. And Mac and Cheese, and Nosy Parker, took the others. As for the grey tom, he sat in the doorway of the miniature chapel, a wreath of snow wrapping his neck.

He gave the people a haughty stare.

'That's a big tom,' said the lady in the fur hat. 'What's his name?'

He doesn't have a name right now,' said Billy. 'There's a suggestion box by the tree. Just fill out one of the papers.'

The street lady pulled a pencil stub from her pocket.

The mayor made his way to the front of the crowd. Cameras snapped. It was his finest moment. 'Clydesdale extends a warm welcome to all you folk from near and far who have come to share in our celebration!' he exclaimed. 'The reopening of High Street chapel has signalled a fresh start for Clydesdale. And Cat Haven is a reminder of our responsibilities. It shows what we can achieve together.'

He pointed skywards. 'The town is looking up!'

People looked up as the boards covering the chapel tower were pulled away. Lucie Morton gasped. She blinked away the snow melting in her eyes. 'Praise be,' she whispered. 'That's the Redemption Bell. They found it. They found our bell.'

The bell rang out across the town.

Billy left the crowd. He pelted down the chapel alley and raced the sound through the deepening dusk.

TWENTY-NINE

The chapel bell was ringing in Christmas.

The carols crossed the chapel yard into the houses of the shops, and the homes of the people. Somewhere in Clydesdale, women dropped their books. Men scratched their heads. Gradually, doors and windows were flung open.

Conga's kits didn't pay any attention. One of them was in the mayor's bedroom, asleep in his shorts. One of them lapped cream on Mrs Davies' fancy dining table. One of them played with Wiggins. The white one curled in the lap of Billy's cat-fearing neighbour.

'Gracie,' the neighbour said. She stroked her new companion. 'My ears are ringing again.'

Billy hit the back stairs of the apartment as the last chime sounded. 'Conga!' he cried. He burst into the kitchen. 'Conga, do you hear that?' He slid to a stop at her feet. 'That's the bell. And you're the one that found it!'

Conga regarded him lazily from the radiator tap. When Billy got down beside her, she stretched. Her paw mussed his hair.

After a bit, the kitchen grew quiet. The last deep tones of the bell faded away.

Conga listened to Billy breathing. She listened to the silence of each snowflake settling on the sill. After a bit, she stuck her rose-petal nose into Billy's ear and hummed.

'Conga,' Billy murmured. He could hardly stay awake. 'Conga, thanks. Thanks a lot.'

ACKNOWLEDGEMENTS

I would like to acknowledge the help and support of Janet Oates, who gave shape to my ramblings, and to Phoebe Sheppard, librarian extraordinaire. My thanks also extend to the volunteers of Homeless Cat Rescue in Toronto, for generously providing information about the feral cat.

AN EXTRACT FROM

Dog Lost

by
Ingrid Lee

Mackenzie lay under his covers in the dark. He counted each flat footstep slamming up the stairs.

One, two, three . . . He pulled his pillow close and peered into the night.

Seven, eight, nine . . . His bones locked.

Eleven, twelve . . . The door swung open. Bright light from the hall invaded his room, and a dark figure walked up to the bed. 'Here,' a voice grunted. 'Tried to cash in my chips and ended up with this for my trouble. Mind you don't let it chew up my shoes.'

A wet lump landed on Mackenzie's bed. Seconds later the door slammed shut. The bedroom was black again.

Mackenzie curled away from the damp weight that trembled on top of the blanket. He could feel hot air whistle past his ear. He could smell fear. And he could make out the splotches of white. When he found the courage to touch one of them, it crumpled in his hand like heavy silk.

It was an ear, a soft silky ear.

Something began to whack his leg. Mackenzie worked it out. A tail was beating against his leg. The prod in his tummy was a paw. And the cold dry poke under his neck, well, that was a nose.

The thing on his bed was a dog. A dog! His father had thrown a dog on the bed.

In the dark Mackenzie lay still, holding the ear lightly. Just as he was getting used to the soft way it folded in his fingers, the dog licked his chin, a slurpy ice-cream lick. Mackenzie slid his hand from the ear to the smooth damp head. He ran his hand on down the neck and curled his fingers into the loose skinny folds. He waited. After a bit the dog stopped trembling and settled into the covers like warm butter. It was going to sleep.

'Cash,' whispered Mackenzie. His father had called the dog Cash. Mackenzie closed his eyes and breathed carefully, breathing in with the dog, breathing out with the dog. He stayed as still as a sleeping boy.

It wasn't that long before he was a sleeping boy.

So that's how Mackenzie and Cash spent their first night together, wrapped up close, nose to nose. In the morning they got quite a surprise when they opened their eyes. Both of them jumped. They didn't know that the other was really there. They thought it was just a dream.

Mackenzie took a good look at the dog lying on his pillow. It yawned, so he got a good look inside and out. It had a long pink tongue and bright brown eyes. And it was a puppy, a girl puppy. Mackenzie was pretty certain about that.

The puppy looked back at Mackenzie. She saw a freckled nose. She looked right into Mackenzie's blue eyes with her big brown ones, and sneezed. She blew spit all over his face.

They both scrambled out of bed.

Mackenzie followed Cash down the stairs. The puppy was in so much of a hurry, her paws slipped on the bare wood and Mackenzie had to grab her tail to slow her down. He pushed her out into the back garden. It was early spring and still chilly, so they both shivered while the puppy did her business. She was as glad as Mackenzie was to get back into the house, especially when the morning train whistled shrilly beyond the fence.

Back in the middle of the kitchen, the puppy looked at Mackenzie and wagged her tail. Where was breakfast?

Mackenzie didn't know what puppies ate for breakfast. Whatever it was, he knew they didn't have it in the house. Finally he gave the puppy a bowl of bran flakes swimming in milk, and a piece of bread and peanut butter. She seemed to like that a lot.

With fifteen minutes to go before the school bus, Mackenzie and Cash climbed back upstairs. Cash didn't know that going up steps was just as tricky as going down. She slipped and knocked her noggin. Mackenzie picked her up and hauled her the rest of the way so she didn't come to any more harm. It was a tough job. The puppy wriggled, and bits and pieces of her kept slipping out of his grasp. It was like trying to hang on to a sack of rubber balls.

When they finally got to Mackenzie's bedroom, Mackenzie took a long look at his new dog. He had to go to school, and he wanted a picture to carry with him all day long. She looked good enough to eat. Her coat was a caramel colour, laced with brown sugar and milk. Next to her nose, where the hair was short, you could see her skin, pink as bubble gum. Mackenzie thought she was going to be a big dog, a beautiful big dog. But right then, she was just a pudding pot of puppy with a wet nose and a plump rump full of wriggles.

All the while Mackenzie was memorising Cash, she was memorising him. She must have liked the way he looked. Her tail wagged the whole time.

Anybody could see they were love-struck.

At the last minute Mackenzie remembered to leave Cash a drink. He filled his old fish bowl at the bathroom sink, letting the water run until it was ice cold. He put some newspapers in the corner too, just in case. Then he gave the puppy a hug and closed his door. 'I'll be back before you know it, Cash,' he called as he ran downstairs. 'We'll go out!'

Cash was asleep under the bedclothes before the school bus got to the end of the road. She hadn't felt so warm and safe for a long time, or so full either. She stuck her pink snout into the pillow, where it still smelled of the boy, and let her belly spread out wider than a jam doughnut.

At school, Mackenzie didn't have it as easy. But he did his best to make the day go by. He wrote a sum on the board and read a poem out loud. In between lessons he thought about Cash. 'I've got a dog,' he thought.

At lunch he cleaned the chalk ledge for his teacher and emptied the recycling bin. 'She's waiting for me,' he thought.

During the music lesson he kept time with the rhythm sticks. 'We'll go to the park,' he decided.

Mackenzie looked out of the window anxiously. The sun was shining. The sky was bluer than a robin's egg.

'I've got a dog named Cash,' he wrote in the corner of his notebook.

SAVING MISSISSIPPI
Cornelia Funke

How can Emma save her horse?

Every holiday, Emma loves helping her grandma Dolly at her animal sanctuary. At home she isn't even allowed a guinea pig. While she's there, Emma's grandma buys her Mississippi, the beloved horse of an old friend, Mr Clipperbush, who has passed away.

Emma can't believe her luck – a horse of her own. But suddenly, there's trouble. Mr Clipperbush's long-lost nephew wants the horse back – and will stop at nothing to get his way.

What can Emma do? Saving Mississippi means everything . . .

. . . plenty of mystery, resourceful children . . . and loveable animals.
THE BOOKSELLER

Paperback, ISBN: 978-1-906427-51-1, £5.99

 Find out more about Chicken House books and authors.
Visit our website: www.doublecluck.com